The Treasure of the River Kwai!

A "Globe Kids" Adventure!

By Doug Gehman

Copyright © 2004
J. Douglas Gehman
All Rights Reserved

All rights reserved. No part of this book may be reproduced in any form, except for the inclusion of brief quotations, without permission in writing from the author or publisher.

Library of Congress
Control Number:

ISBN 0-9765168-1-0

First printing • January 2005

Additional copies of this book are available by mail. Send $10.00 each (tax and postage extra) to:

Globe Publishing
P.O. Box 3040
Pensacola, FL 32516-3040
850.453.3453
www.gme.org

Published by
J. Douglas Gehman
Globe Publishing

Dedication

To my Dad,
James Robert Gehman,
who always encouraged me to serve God and
pursue my dreams. He inspired me with his own
forms of creativity, always inventing, and always
making his world more beautiful. Whether at work
in his gardens and groves, tinkering in his shop,
or digging out new gems of truth from the Bible,
Dad lived his life joyfully because of Jesus.

About the Author and the Book

Doug and his wife Beth Ann first went to Asia as independent missionaries in 1978. During their fifteen years on the mission field, they served extensively in Taiwan, Thailand, Malaysia, India and Sri Lanka.

Three of their four children were born in Asia.

For seven years they lived in Hua Hin, Thailand, on the western coast of the Gulf of Thailand. Much of the content of this book drew its inspiration from those years. While this story is fictitious, there is some evidence that, during World War II, Japanese occupation forces hid gold in the mountains near the River Kwai. Many have searched, but no gold has ever been found.

Doug attended Goshen College and Fuller Theological Seminary, and earned Master's and Doctorate degrees in Missions at Liberty Christian University.

Doug serves as President and Director of Globe Missionary Evangelism in Pensacola, Florida. Globe, a non-denominational missions sending agency, and its affiliates oversee more than 200 missionaries in 35 nations.

Doug and Beth have ministered in over 40 nations.

Chapter 1

THE CAVE

"Kevin! Over here! Look at this!" David Carson leaned his tall, lean frame carefully on the gray cavern wall. The tips of his sneakers tempted the edge of a deep, dark precipice. He bent over the edge pointing his flashlight into the black hole and strained his eyes to see something, anything, but the cavern blackness engulfed the white beam only twenty-five feet down. The hole was much deeper. David kicked a stone into the mouth and waited, listening.

A moment passed before the faint sound of a splash echoed from the depths far below. Standing tall for his eighteen years, David clung to the cave wall and leaned tentatively over the edge trying in vain to urge the light beam a little deeper into the emptiness.

The Treasure of the River Kwai

"Hey, Kevin!" David waited until an impatient, "What!!?" echoed back. "Come over here and take a look at this hole!"

Kevin Merritt, who was searching out of view across the darkened room of the cave, emerged from the shadows. "Get that flashlight out of my face, man!" David pointed the beam into the hole as Kevin hustled over. He stood beside David and they both strained their eyes downward into the black void.

"Whhhhhooooooooaaa, man! That is a killer hole!" Kevin edged his short, muscular frame carefully nearer to the crusty edge. He leaned over, aiming his light, and looked down. Gravel crunched under his sneakers and then fell silently into the abyss.

Kevin's flashlight, larger and with a stronger beam than David's, pushed light another fifteen feet down, but still they could not stretch the pale rays into the depths to the bottom. "How far down is it?"

"My guess, at least 75 feet. I kicked a stone in and it took a second or so to hit bottom. It splashed into water, so I figure it must be the sea down there. Maybe there's a natural exit into the Gulf."

David stood up and moved his flashlight beam around the cave. They were in the small anteroom off a larger, higher chamber. The ante-room was cramped and the ceiling very low; a narrow ledge around the hole was the only walking space. David noticed that by clinging to the cave wall one could maneuver all the way around the hole. But he didn't want to try it without ropes. The

The Treasure of the River Kwai

ceiling in the ante-room was just above David's head, and small, uneven rock forms jutted down at them.

Feeling his blonde hair brush against a protruding bump, David put his hand on the ceiling and backed away from the hole. Vertigo, the confused height-induced sensation in the eyes, challenged his balance. He wanted to get away from that black edge. David looked at Kevin beside him. Resisting the queasy feeling he joked, "Think we should climb down?" A note of daring in David's voice didn't fully hide his fear. Kevin didn't look up. His eyes eagerly probed the chasm's depths.

"Right." With ropes and gear, better shoes, and stronger flashlights the two boys would be on their way without hesitation. But they had been in the cave for over an hour, their flashlights were beginning to dim, and they had no climbing equipment. Good sense, born of David's missionary upbringing in Asia, tethered his youthful appetite for risk. The dimming light from their flashlights pressed them to leave the cave.

"I want to see what's down there," Kevin said. He looked at the ledge surrounding the hole. At one point on the opposite side of the hole near the cave wall, the ledge widened and jutted out over the hole. By climbing around the ledge and lying down on the wide area he figured he could easily look in and maybe see farther down. But, the ledge leading to it was narrow and hard to reach. Kevin leaned his back against the rough, dry rock and edged along the narrow shelf toward the ledge.

The Treasure of the River Kwai

"What are you doing, you idiot!?" David yelled. "You need a rope to do that! I don't feel like scraping your carcass off the bottom!"

"Relax! It's not as hard as it looks." Kevin reached the wide ledge and dropped to his knees. He lay down on the rock and edged his body horizontally out onto the ledge. In this position he hung dangerously over the hole. Belly down and straddling the narrow ledge, he let his arms dangle freely into the abyss. One hand clung to his flashlight. Kevin eased forward on his stomach until his head pushed over the edge. Now he had a clear view straight down into the hole. He pointed his flashlight directly down, and this time the light beam probed deeper. He moved the yellow beam around searching the murky depths. David stood tentatively across the hole from Kevin, watching. He leaned against the cave wall and shined his light nervously on his friend.

"This rock is rough!" Kevin squirmed to get more comfortable. "Shoot!" His legs, too long to stretch out on the short ledge, crammed against the cave wall behind him. "It's digging into my chest!" He squirmed again, and almost dropped his flashlight. Rocks crumbled loose, fell silently away, and crashed into the water a moment later.

David winced and shouted, "Way to go, ace! Go ahead and fall in! What exactly are you trying to do?" David shifted position, checking his footing near the hole, intuitively conscious of his own safety. He watched, keeping his flashlight trained on Kevin. Always the most cautious of the pair, David began to regret showing Kevin the hole. Kevin was

The Treasure of the River Kwai

more aggressive about adventure. His gutsy nerve had endangered them more than once, a fact that frustrated David and yet made him admire Kevin. The differences enhanced their friendship.

"I want to see what's in this hole!" Kevin, lying flat and uncomfortable on his chest, steadied the flashlight beam down the gray, stone walls. Both boys strained their eyes to see through the feeble glimmer of light.

"Wow! I *can* see all the way down there!" He waved the ghostly light beam around slowly. "There's water down there! And the hole gets bigger at the bottom!"

"Like I said, I kicked a stone in and it hit water," David said. "What'dya mean, it gets bigger at the bottom?"

"You know, the walls don't go straight down all the way. They widen out way down there." Kevin moved the beam around and found something on the opposite wall at the bottom. "It almost looks like another tunnel down, like where the water comes in or something." The flashlight beam flickered on and off. He pulled it up and banged on it. "You got any more batteries? This thing is dying!"

"Nope. I only got my own, and they're dying too. We better get going or we'll run out of light before we get out." David shook his light too, trying to coax brightness out of the dimming light. Cautious but not easily intimidated, David calculated how much light they had left. They had to walk at least five minutes to daylight. "Come on. Let's get going."

Kevin ignored him, shook his flashlight, and again scanned the bottom of the hole. "Man, this

The Treasure of the River Kwai

is awesome!" The light beam passed over a large object. "There's something down there!" Kevin slapped his flashlight hard, and this time it went out. He hit it again and it flickered on, brighter. Pointing the beam down, he trained it again on the faint object. "There *is* something down there! What is that thing?"

"It's probably some wet rocks or some mineral deposit from the cave. Maybe the flashlight is glaring off it," David offered, impatient to get going.

"No way. It's got some kind of definite shape, but I can't make it out." He stretched the light down hard with his extended arm, squinting his eyes. "Turn your flashlight off, David. It's glaring into my eyes."

David clicked his light off. Kevin's flashlight beam settled again on the object, and then he could see it—the oval shape of a small dingy. "It's a boat! Yeah, that's what it is. It's a boat, like a little rowboat or something! It's even got some oars in it! Jeez, what's a boat doing in this cave?" Kevin looked up and they both stared at each other in astonishment.

"Then there is passageway out to the Gulf down there!" David said with growing excitement. "How else could someone get a boat in here?" The discovery momentarily made David forget his eagerness to leave. In vain he leaned over the edge trying to catch a glimpse of the boat.

"Man, this is neat!" Kevin said, turning his light back down to the dingy. "Can you see that down there?" He stretched his right arm down into the hole, and leaned far over the ledge trying to get a better look.

The Treasure of the River Kwai

Seeing Kevin's dangerous position, David yelled, "You're crazy, man! Knock it off!" David leaned over the side of the precipice trying to see. "I can't see anything from here." David pulled away from the hole. "You better get off that ledge before I do see something—like your butt falling to the bottom of this hole."

David waited a moment for Kevin to respond. He turned his flashlight back on and shook it. "Come on. Let's go." He said. "If our lights die it won't matter what's down there. We'll be two skeletons up here gazing into the hole forever. We can come back tomorrow." David subdued his own excitement and made the responsible decision. His friend ignored the urging. "Let's come back tomorrow, Kevin," David repeated.

Kevin reluctantly pulled himself to his knees and sat on the ledge. He scratched his short-cropped black hair. "We've got to get some more stuff. Some rope and big waterproof flashlights. Definitely extra batteries." He glared at his flashlight in disgust, and shook it again. It flickered. "Then we can come back tomorrow." He pointed his flashlight directly into David's face. "How about it?"

David squinted impatiently at the light. "Yeah, like I said already. We can come back tomorrow. Let's get out of here before we have to feel our way all the way back."

Kevin stood up, brushed dirt off his knees and khaki shorts, and maneuvered back around edge of the hole. The pair began picking their way toward the room's left passageway. The other tunnel, discovered by Kevin earlier, was lower and narrower.

The Treasure of the River Kwai

That would be explored tomorrow. Kevin looked at it longingly as they passed. "I checked out that tunnel over there. It goes way in and then down real steep."

As they left the large room and entered the tunnel leading out of the cave, with Kevin mumbling about supplies they should buy, David reached up and felt the ceiling of the passage. It was dry. He figured the small island they were on had no natural water supply, so the whole cave was probably dry down to sea level. The cave was cooler than the outside air, but not cold like caves in America. Compared to South Thailand's humid, tropical sun outside, the cave's rock provided interior shade and made the temperature bearable. But the boys could feel the air steadily warming as they ascended upward to the cave entrance.

They walked a hundred feet in silence. The passage narrowed as they approached the cave mouth. It was June, the beginning of Thailand's monsoon season. For the next six months regular rains would dampen most of the nation. Although the rains brought welcome relief from Thailand's sweltering hot season, the increased humidity usually countered the cooler temperatures. Today no rain had fallen and the sun's heat bore mercilessly down on the island chain of Anthong National Marine Park.

The tropical sun threw warm shadows on the walls of the cave as the boys rounded the final corner toward the exit, and with a mixture of relief and excitement, they walked the final steps to the outside.

Chapter 2

Island of the Sleeping Cow

Emerging into the daylight, David and Kevin stood briefly in the hot sun, enjoying the brightness of the tropical sun after the dark environment of the cave. But the balmy heat quickly drove them to shade beneath the nearby brush growth. As they stood in silence, David thought about his folks in Bangkok, four hundred miles to the north.

David brushed his blond hair out of his eyes and said, "Man, I'll have to call my folks tonight and tell them about this cave." For nearly twenty years the Carson's had lived in Thailand, serving as missionaries to the Thai people. David was born in the OMF Mission Hospital in Central Thailand, and, except for several furloughs in the United States, had lived his entire life in tropical Asia. He spoke

The Treasure of the River Kwai

Thai fluently. His obvious white features, which would forever mark him as a foreigner in this land, didn't change how he felt about Asia. Thailand was definitely home.

David and Kevin met at Dalat School, a missionary boarding school in Penang, Malaysia, three hundred miles to the south. Dalat had been a good experience for David. He had attended since third grade. At first it was hard being separated from his parents. However, three one-month vacations every year made life bearable, and now that he was older it seemed normal to be away. He had made a lot of friends, enjoyed his teachers and "house parents," and generally adjusted to life at boarding school. His teenage years brought more independence so things were easier. During his years in junior high and high school, like many missionary kids who were forced to develop self-reliance early, he had survived and then thrived on the experience. He got along well with his parents, looked forward to seeing them on vacation, which is what he had been doing before this adventure with Kevin. But now, on this first non-essential trip away from home, he was spreading his adult wings.

Friends like Kevin helped a lot. David realized that without Dalat School and the other students, the only American culture he could know was what he learned from his parents, the family's short visits "home," and an occasional video or television show. In real life experience, he only knew Thailand and Malaysia. At Dalat School he had learned how to relate to American guys like Kevin. And then there were the girls . . . especially Kate. . . .

The Treasure of the River Kwai

He liked Thailand and had Thai friends, but being a white, blond-haired, blue-eyed, foreigner made it abundantly clear to everyone that he was not Thai. So David had learned the basics about how to live with the inherent contradictions of life as a foreigner. He was aware that many kids who were raised on the mission field struggled with their identity, so he was glad he knew who he was.

"The sun feels great. I guess we were getting a little claustrophobic in there," Kevin said. David nodded, jarred from his thoughts.

Kevin continued, "Did you feel the air pushing up through the hole? I'll bet there's an opening down there and air is being moved around from the water and wind moving in and out of the bottom opening." The idea excited Kevin. "Maybe tomorrow we should take the boat around the island and look for a beach entrance. If we check our position here, and figure where the hole is, we can probably come close to where it might be."

David stretched and scratched at an itchy spot on his back. His white T-shirt felt damp from the tropical heat and he instinctively began checking for ants on the ground or in the bushes behind him. He pulled his T-shirt out of his cut-off jeans and replied, "Yeah, that might work."

David stepped out of the shade, grabbed his small backpack from under the bush where he had stashed it. He shoved in his flashlight. He shaded his blue eyes with one hand and scanned the distant islands of Anthong Park. From the pinnacle where they stood he could clearly see the beautiful array of bulbous green atolls that formed this 50-island

The Treasure of the River Kwai

archipelago. Little islands, with tufts of green growing out of gray rock, were sprinkled over blue sea. The sun, lower than before, glistened off the water.

He pulled his eyes away and looked around. Behind him, hidden in a wall of rock, the small cave opening descended into the bowels of the island. The mouth of the cave was almost totally hidden in rocky crags. David opened his pack, found his water bottle, and drank lustily. Finishing, he offered the bottle to Kevin, "You want some?"

"Yeah, man! I'm thirsty." Kevin took a long drink and almost drained the bottle. Handing it back, he said, "I'm hungry too."

"Yeah, let's get going." He took Kevin's flashlight, stuffed it in the pack, and threw the pack on his back. David walked to the edge of the rounded top plateau and looked toward Koh Samui, *Samui Island* in the Thai language, 19 miles away. The sun, now behind him as it descended to the west in the afternoon sky, painted glorious colors of blue on the tropical water. David could see Koh Samui in the distance to the southeast. It was only 37 square miles in size, small by most standards, but a giant compared to the other islands of Anthong.

David scanned the nearer islands. Anthong's numerous little islands huddled closely together were a geographical part of Koh Samui. But the park marked them as a unit, by their nearness to each other and distance from the other islands. Most islands were covered with scrub tropical foliage at the top growing out of rocky limestone cliffs below. Some were only rock. Many cliffs dropped straight into the water. Few sandy beaches existed in Anthong

The Treasure of the River Kwai

Park. One exception was the beach on Koh Nua Ta Lap, *Island of the Sleeping Cow*, the main island of Anthong. David and Kevin would return there.

David enjoyed looking at the sea. This part of the Gulf of Thailand offered some of the most delightful beaches and water in the world. Multiple shades of blue, painted by the sun, charmed the eyes. Each shade revealed a different depth of water. Dark blue water was the deepest. Lighter shades, reflecting the bottom, indicated shallower depths. Brilliant turquoise near the shoreline meant white sand below. And because these waters were unspoiled by sediment or man-made pollution, a snorkel-equipped swimmer could easily see details on the bottom even when depths exceeded 50 feet.

David crossed over to another part of the plateau. "We better get going," he said, not really to Kevin. "Yeah," came the reply. "Especially if we must buy some stuff to come back tomorrow. We gotta go back to Samui tonight."

Looking down, David examined the return route to their small rented motorboat. Earlier in the day David and Kevin had climbed steep rocks from the beach to reach the cave entrance. This island, like many others in the chain, was not more than five hundred feet across. Its edges, all around, were cliffs rising straight up out of the water. Kevin and David had to climb directly out of their boat onto the rock face. They secured the boat onto a small tree that clung boldly to the cliff face. The sheer cliffs jutted skyward and rounded near the top. It made the island look like a gray and green cupcake. Although there was almost no sand or dirt to be found on

The Treasure of the River Kwai

the entire island, the small trees and shrubs found secure hold in porous rock at the top. Some, like the one to which their boat was tied, gripped the cliff face. These bushes the boys had used as hand holds to climb the cliff from the boat.

The afternoon sun slowly descended to the west as the boys climbed down toward their rented boat. They would drive the boat south to Koh Nua Ta Lap. They had considered staying the night in a bungalow at Koh Nua Ta Lap but now, with their discovery of the dingy in the cave, they needed to catch the ferry to Koh Samui where they could buy additional supplies.

Conscious of the time, David and Kevin hurried carefully down the sides of the cliff. David untied the boat from its mooring, while Kevin jerked the two-cycle motor to life. Seating themselves quickly, they headed toward the ferry at Koh Nua Ta Lap. The short ride home was uneventful, with the afternoon sun steadily falling toward the water and glaring into the corner of their eyes.

As they pulled into the dock at Koh Nua Ta Lap Kevin said, "Hey, we better not tell anyone about that cave. Let's just keep it a secret for now, or we'll have everyone and his brother following us over there tomorrow." David agreed.

As they tied up their boat at the dock the frail old man, from whom they had rented the boat that morning, shuffled over. They paid him the balance for the day and negotiated a price to rent the boat again. As expected, the inquisitive old man, jabbering in the southern Thai dialect, asked about their excursion. He wondered if they had found anything interesting.

The Treasure of the River Kwai

Kevin was eager to talk about their discovery, but, hearing of the man's inquiry from David, feigned weariness from a day in the sun. He shook his head. David smiled and simply told the man, "Koh suay mahk" (the islands are very beautiful).

They walked toward the ferry. "Man, this isn't going to be easy keeping quiet." David mused. "It's like buying a new car and then having to keep it in the garage for a month. Gag!"

Kevin laughed, "Yeah, I know what you mean. But I guess we haven't really found anything yet anyway. Just an old boat in a cave. Just keep telling yourself that." They decided to call Kevin's parents. "We'll tell them we found a neat cave and want to explore some more," Kevin suggested.

Then David remembered. "Wichai," he muttered to himself.

"What?" Kevin looked at David as they walked.

"I just remembered, Wichai. You know, my Thai friend I told you about. He might be coming down from Bangkok to meet us. I totally forgot until now. He called me before I left and I invited him to come along, but he couldn't. But then he called back and said he would come. He might be at the bungalow when we get back there."

"Should we tell him about the cave?" Kevin asked, a little suspicious. He didn't know Wichai. Kevin was still new to Thai culture and had not made any Thai friends. And like most people, Kevin was instinctively cautious about "foreigners." All those unfamiliar customs and the strange language. It had not yet fully occurred to Kevin that it he was who was the foreigner in Thailand.

The Treasure of the River Kwai

"Oh yeah," David said reassuringly. "Wichai and I practically grew up together. He speaks English, so you'll be able to talk to him too. He's cool." Having grown up in a cross-cultural environment—and tired from the day's activities—David did not notice Kevin's hesitation.

Kevin shrugged and nodded, "OK." Kevin was also apprehensive about the addition of a third person into their adventure. He wondered if, when Wichai joined them, he would become the odd-man in the trio. But as they left the dock, Kevin decided to accept the possibility and deal with it.

He was getting used to the occasional strange feelings that come with living in a foreign country, but it still wasn't always easy. Especially at Dalat School, most of the missionary kids knew another language and they'd frequently joke around with it. Or use it for private conversations, excluding all other hearers—including him.

There were a bunch of kids who spoke Thai, others who knew Bahasa Malaysia or Bahasa Indonesia, a few who spoke Nepali, Bengali and some of the languages of India. Kevin spoke only English and it made him feel stupid. He compensated by being a show-off.

Many of the kids ate all the local food variations, and mixed well with the national students. Kevin still had to work at it. And David. Jeez, he could do anything. David was his friend, but sometimes it just seemed David was always one step ahead of him, especially in the friendship thing.

Kevin had come to Thailand with his parents less than a year before. They lived in Surat Thani, on

The Treasure of the River Kwai

Thailand's southern peninsula, not far from where they were. Kevin's Dad worked for USAID doing research at a Thai shrimp farm outside Surat Thani. Kevin had first met David at Dalat last August. Now that David was spending the beginning of their summer vacation in the Merritt home, the boys had decided to explore the Anthong Island chain for a few days.

Surat Thani was a principal city of south Thailand, on the narrow southerly peninsula that Thailand shared with Burma and Malaysia. The peninsula was created by two bodies of water—the Indian Ocean to the west, and to the east the tranquil waters of the Gulf of Thailand. The peninsula formed Thailand's distinctive shape on the map: the head of an elephant. As Italy is known for its boot shape, Thailand is famous in Asia for its resemblance to an elephant's head. Surat Thani, located halfway down the elephant's nose, was the main launching point for travel to Koh Samui.

The chain of islands called Anthong was near the western shores of the Gulf. Even on this outer island the boys were only about 50 miles from Kevin's home. To get to Koh Samui they had first taken a bus to Don Sak Village on the coast. They then boarded a ferry and sailed 20 miles to Koh Samui. At Nathon, Koh Samui's main town, they rented a room. The next day they caught another ferry to Koh Nua Ta Lap.

Now back after a tiring day of exploring, the boys made their way to another dock to wait for the ferry to Koh Samui. "We've got about forty-five minutes before the ferry leaves," David said. "If it leaves on time."

The Treasure of the River Kwai

They walked up the ramp from the dock. He checked his watch and noted the time was 4:15 p.m.

The boys walked along the dusty, litter-filled street and found a small outdoor restaurant near the water's edge. They sat down under a faded beach umbrella and ordered two Cokes each.

Drinking the Cokes refreshed them—and made them hungry. They suddenly felt famished.

"Gosh, I'm starving! Can we get something to eat around here?" Kevin turned on his chair and looked around. Little wooden shop houses, pressed together along the street, offered sparse possibilities to his hungry American eyes. The boys decided to wait until they returned to Koh Samui to eat dinner. "I don't know if we'll get much better there. I'm hungry for a hamburger!"

"Get ready to pay for it," David said. "If we eat some rice and seafood, it'll be cheap, but if you want a real hamburger we'll have to go to the big hotels, and then it'll cost ya."

They finished their drinks then walked to the ferry. David bought some dried barbecued squid from a lady hawker. She was pushing a two-wheeled cart the top of which was covered by the odd-looking sea creature. Another hawker was selling roasted pork and chicken on little sticks. Kevin bought about ten sticks of meat. The old woman put them in a plastic bag. Munching on their Asian delicacies, they walked toward the ferry launch and arrived at the dock as the ferry pulled in from Koh Samui. This was the boat's last circuit for the day.

Boarding the small ferry they noticed it was the same ancient craft they had used in the morning.

The Treasure of the River Kwai

It was a diesel-powered, wooden boat with dirty, faded paint. Blue smoke belched incessantly from the pounding engine. About twenty people, including several other white tourists, boarded with them. After fifteen minutes of loading, in which a variety of baskets, boxes, tied up bundles and other things were thrown helter-skelter onto the deck by chattering Thai workers, they finally pushed off from the dock. The boat chugged unevenly, spit a plume of thick blue smoke, and turned toward Koh Samui, leaving a faint oily trail in its watery wake.

The boys settled uncomfortably on a pile of ropes at the stern and looked north, squinting to see their island and its mysterious cave. It was hidden from view. After a few minutes weariness and heat exhaustion overcame them and their heads nodded. There they rested for the duration of the 19-mile journey to Koh Samui.

David dreamily dozed while the ferry chugged and smoked. He figured Wichai would find them when they got to Nathon. It shouldn't be too hard for them to find each other. Nathon was not much of a town by international tourist standards. No tall buildings, only a few real streets. A quiet and quaint beach town. It was a great place to relax and enjoy the beach and natural beauty of the tropics. David had noticed when they arrived yesterday how many more western tourists were on the island this year compared to the last time he had visited three years before on family vacation.

"I think we should take all our stuff with us tomorrow and stay at that bungalow on Koh Nua Ta Lap tomorrow night." Kevin lifted his head as

The Treasure of the River Kwai

the ferry approached the palm covered shore line of Koh Samui. He looked at David for a response and then turned his head to look over the water at the town. The buildings of Nathon blended charmingly into the tropical seascape. Many roofs were quaintly thatched; some had modern tiles or flat roofs, but not a single modern building rose above the heights of the trees. "At least if we have our stuff we can stay if we want to. Then we can explore another day before we have to go home," Kevin continued.

"I guess we could get the room when we get there in the morning," David wondered. "I don't know if I feel like dragging our packs with us to the island."

"Right." Kevin hadn't thought of that. "Whatever."

Arriving at Nathon, the ferry pulled lazily up to the wooden dock. A deckhand threw a line and dock worker lashed the boat to the pier. A rickety gang-plank was laid across and the passengers, David and Kevin among them, grabbed belongings and climbed off the boat. The boys went quickly to Harbor Road where they turned south and walked to their bungalow. They emerged an hour later feeling refreshed and rejuvenated after a shower and change of clothes.

As they descended the stairs of the little house, a young Thai man approached. He was thin and short next to Kevin and David, but of normal height and weight for a Thai. His jet-black hair was disheveled from the long voyage by bus and ferry. He was carrying a backpack. David immediately recognized his Bangkok friend and grinned and waved. "Hey, Wichai!"

Chapter 3
Trouble in Kanchanaburi

While David and his friends prepared for their second expedition to Anthong Park, events were unfolding in the city of Kanchanaburi northwest of Bangkok that were wholly unrelated to the boys but would ultimately have serious consequences for their plans.

In the heart of Kanchanaburi's old residential district, two men sat cheerlessly drinking whiskey under the shaded porch of an aged wooden house. The first was a wiry Thai man named Somsuk Witonah, twenty-four years old, with short-cropped hair and a scar on his face. The scar ran from his left ear, across his cheek, and down to his chin. A quick-witted man, Somsuk had a way with words and personal style that, except for the glaring and

The Treasure of the River Kwai

offensive scar, quickly endeared him to people. He had learned that people thought the scar less heinous when he explained that a dog attacked him when he was young. In reality he had earned the scar in a bar room fight.

The oldest of five children, his father had left home and disappeared when he was ten, leaving his mother alone to care for the family. This she did with little success and promptly fell into drunkenness and the attendance of numerous strange men in the house. Somsuk left home at fourteen and quickly found creative ways to support himself, most of which were illegal. For a short time, after being caught burglarizing a house, he was confined to a juvenile facility. He escaped and stayed clear of the law for three years until he was again arrested for robbing and beating up an old man and his wife in their home. For that crime he spent two years in prison. Since this last release Somsuk had been in constant trouble, often with accompanying violence for which he was prone, but he had managed to remain just beyond the reach of the police.

Somsuk sat across the table from his accomplice in crime, a fat young man named Kauwee who stared blankly into his whiskey glass. Kauwee shifted on his large backside, scratched his belly and mumbled something about wanting food. He smoked incessantly, lighting one cigarette with the butt of the previous one. He seemed constantly to be trying to scratch some unreachable spot on his rotund torso. Kauwee Satrelerdramin was short, round-headed, twenty-six years old and 260 pounds. Kauwee's head was covered by a curly

The Treasure of the River Kwai

black mass of hair that hung uncombed on his forehead and over his ears. His clothes, a grimy T-shirt that strained over his large belly, and gray pants that fit too tightly, punctuated his obnoxious appearance.

Kauwee's home life was similar to Somsuk's. He had quit school and left his fatherless home at the age of thirteen when he discovered he could make more money stealing than he could ever hope to make with an education and legitimate work. For more than ten years, except for three that he spent in a Bangkok jail for larceny, he had done well, he thought. If asked to show anything for his labors, Kauwee could not have done so, because he had wasted most of his illegal earnings in riotous living. But he figured there was always more money to be made in crime, so his prospects were good.

Nowadays the two men made their living working for local Kanchanaburi mafia bosses running drugs and other illegal contraband to Bangkok. They weren't clever enough to be entrusted with big money operations, but what they made, in their opinion, was better than an equal amount they could earn slaving away in rice fields or carrying bricks at a construction site. Like Somsuk, Kauwee enjoyed living outside of the law; unlike Somsuk, Kauwee didn't talk much. Kauwee was big and could do the harder work that Somsuk despised, such as lugging around suitcases full of drugs. These qualities of character, if they could be called that, made possible a perverse but mostly harmonious arrangement between the two criminals, and as such they enjoyed working together.

The Treasure of the River Kwai

The pair occasionally transported drugs and collected small pay-offs that they returned to their bosses in Kanchanaburi, but rarely were they trusted with any significant amounts of money. On other occasions, special couriers who were sent from Kanchanaburi specifically to collect larger pay-offs, met them in Bangkok at various delivery points. Each large delivery to Bangkok earned Somsuk and Kauwee about $100, paid in Baht, the Thailand currency. By making on average several large and small trips per week they could earn more money then they could ever dream of making as a laborer, so overall they were content. Each week, after completing their delivery and collecting their pay they returned to their wooden house in Kanchanaburi. The remainder of their week was spent hanging around local bars or seeking out the city's illicit pleasures, which were not difficult to find, for Kanchanaburi was known for its gambling, prostitution and other vices.

But today Somsuk and Kauwee sat in the front of their wooden house, depressed and afraid, although neither would openly admit these emotions to the other. During their last trip to Bangkok something had gone terribly wrong. An informant's tip had resulted in their bus being stopped at a police checkpoint in the suburbs of Bangkok. Passengers were ordered off the bus while special drug agents with dogs inspected the luggage. Seeing that they were about to be caught, Somsuk and Kauwee quietly slipped to the back of the growing crowd of passengers and curious pedestrians and escaped the police net.

The Treasure of the River Kwai

They were at first delighted to have avoided arrest, but when they returned to Kanchanaburi and reported to their bosses what had happened they quickly learned the ruthless nature of the drug business. They were given exactly two weeks, half of which time had already passed, to return the drugs or their value. They had to find 300,000 Baht (about $12,000 in Thai currency), or face "penalties," which they knew meant certain death. So on this day they sat in the shade of their house, drinking and trying to formulate a plan. Between their gulps of whiskey, Kauwee sat in his chair chain smoking, while Somsuk paced back and forth in the dirt, combing a hand through his hair and mumbling Thai vulgarities. They were both soon drunk and in this dazed condition their minds searched for a solution:

We could borrow the money to settle the debt, and then repay the loan over the next few years or so. They dismissed this idea when they realized no institution, including the illegal ones, would loan them any money.

We can go to Bangkok and rob a gold or jewelry store. The idea had merit, but they had no experience with this kind of job and time was too short to plan. Besides they had no guns. Trying to get one now, even through illegal means, would clearly give away their plans.

How about we rob one of the other drug carriers in the gang, and return that delivery as our own? Somsuk figured if they did it right the other carriers would not know who had stung them. But then he remembered that their common boss, or one of the

The Treasure of the River Kwai

affiliates, would be immediately suspicious when Somsuk and Kauwee came into possession of a drug cache right after two others had lost them. So they dropped this idea too.

Let's go search for gold at the River Kwai. This idea was Kauwee's and at first Somsuk rejected it knowing no one had found any gold in almost a year of searching. But Kauwee, in a rare show of insight, added, "If we don't find any gold we can just disappear into the jungles because that is where we'll have to hide anyway," and so the decision was made.

The two men, energized by the new idea and want of time, jumped to their feet and began assembling the things they would need for a trip into the jungles near the River Kwai Bridge. They figured they must first go to Bangkok to get inside information about the latest searches, for no one in Kanchanaburi was willing to talk about gold to known thugs. They made a few arrangements, packed belongings for the trip, gathered what money they had stashed away, and mounted a bus for Bangkok.

Chapter 4

The Map Key

"Davy! I've been looking for you!"

After the long bus ride to Surat, Wichai was glad to see his old friend. Wichai had never met the other American standing with David, but David had often talked about a friend name Kevin, which in Wichai's attempts at pronunciation, came out *Keewin. This must be Keewin,* Wichai thought. Wichai understood David's need to connect with his own people. Growing up together in Bangkok, Wichai and David had become close. Differences, which seemed minor when they were young, but about which they were more aware as teenagers, still hadn't affected Wichai and David's friendship. Some of the American young people Wichai knew wouldn't hang out with him now. David was different.

The Treasure of the River Kwai

He was glad David could speak Thai. His English was OK, but between the two they could talk about almost anything and understand each other. And both learned something. Wichai had never been to America. His brother went to Seattle to study, but he had decided on a Thai university. David provided most of what Wichai knew about the United States, and the American people. Most of the Americans he had met were difficult to understand. They were loud and impolite, sometimes even vulgar, the way they'd walk right into your home with dirty shoes on their feet. David was different. *Except for his blonde hair, he was almost Thai.*

He walked up to the pair, smiling broadly. David slapped Wichai on the back, glad to see him. The two jokingly poked at each other.

"I remembered you were coming. I hope you haven't been waiting long." David said in flawless Thai. "Did you have a good trip down?"

Wichai reverted to his native tongue and said, "Yeah. Just a long trip on the bus. I talked to your folks and they said you were still in Surat Thani. They gave me your friend's phone number so I called but they said you had left already. I figured I'd probably be able to find you here."

Kevin looked tentatively at Wichai. Not knowing him, and not being able to speak Thai, he felt awkward. He wondered again how this was going to work. This time David sensed Kevin's apprehension and said in English, "Wichai, this is my friend Kevin. His parents are the people you called in Surat. I met Kevin at Dalat School this year. He lives in Surat Thani."

The Treasure of the River Kwai

   Wichai nodded politely, but hesitated momentarily about how to greet Kevin. The proper Thai greeting is the Wai: a person brings his hands together as in prayer in front of his face, with the extended fingers placed just above chin level and bows slightly to the other. Wichai was familiar with the American handshake, but he didn't know if Kevin, being in Thailand, knew the wai. And being a typical Thai Wichai restrained from being too assertive. The boys stared briefly at each other, both hesitating.
   Kevin said hello, and stood with his hands at his sides. David sensed the awkwardness and looked at Kevin. "Wichai and I have been close friends since we were five years old. We kind of grew up together in Bangkok. He's going to the Ramkhanheng University there now . . ." David's voice sort of drifted off, and then he added, "And he loves to explore!"
   With that word, Kevin looked at David and smiled. He extended his hand, "Glad to meet you, Wichai. We've had an exciting day exploring, for sure." Kevin stuck out his hand, Wichai grabbed it they shook and smiled.
   "Where did you go?" Wichai asked as the trio walked toward the restaurant.
   David said, "We were on an island in Anthong and found a neat cave. I don't know if anyone else really knows it's there. Way inside the cave we found a hole that dropped down to the sea. There was a boat at the bottom of the hole, so that's how we knew it was the sea. We figure there is no other way that boat could have gotten in there except through

The Treasure of the River Kwai

a water entrance. Maybe there's something else in there. At least it's worth exploring more."

Wichai's eyes grew wide with excitement as David related more details of the story. They stopped walking. Kevin stood across from David and listened, watching Wichai's reaction.

"Woooooo, Davy! This is amazing! You won't believe this! I just heard a story last week about a lost treasure map, hidden by pirates on an island in south Thailand over 50 years ago!"

"Right." Kevin said sarcastically. "Pirates in 1945. Get real, man."

Wichai looked at Kevin, not understanding the sarcasm. To David he said, "You remember about a year ago the big excitement in Kanchanaburi near the River Kwai Bridge when all those people went looking for a lost gold treasure?"

David nodded and said, "Yeah?"

"All the newspapers covered it for over six months," Wichai continued. "An old Thai lady said she had a map, given to her by a Japanese soldier during World War Two that showed the location of a huge treasure of gold the Japanese had stolen from Burma and Singapore. She said they hid it all in a jungle cave near Kanchanaburi during the building of the Bridge over the River Kwai."

"Yeah, I remember the story," David said with rising interest. "What does that have to do with a cave in Anthong?"

"Yeah, and pirates? During World War Two? Come on!" Kevin added, disbelieving.

"The pirate part is true, Kevin." David said. "The Gulf of Thailand has been infested with Thai and

The Treasure of the River Kwai

Malaysian pirates, even right up to recent years. There aren't so many nowadays, because of military patrols, but even ten years ago Thai officials often warned tourists not to venture out in the Gulf alone in small boats because they could be boarded and robbed by pirates. Sometimes they even raped the women on board.

"It was a big problem in the 70s after the Vietnam War during the Vietnamese boat people thing. You know, all those refugees that fled Viet Nam by boat. Many of them carried their life savings in gold and silver stuffed in their luggage and clothes, so when the pirates found them they often robbed and killed them. Sometimes they took the young girls and kept them on their ships and raped them over and over. My folks helped with some refugee stuff when they first came to the field, so they heard horror stories from the survivors. It was bad. The pirates are modern, with motorized boats and stuff. They're not like Blackbeard and Captain Hook, but they still exist. Basically they're just thieves on boats."

Amazed at the coincidence and adventure unfolding before them, the boys walked to the restaurant, talking about caves and treasure. They ordered several Thai seafood dishes and rice for three, and listened as Wichai continued. "During the Japanese occupation of Thailand in the Second World War, Japanese soldiers saved up a huge cache of gold from looting neighbor countries. The story says they hid a part of their treasure in a cave near the River Kwai Bridge project. One of the soldiers gave a copy of the map to his Thai girlfriend, who,

The Treasure of the River Kwai

after the soldier died in an explosion at the bridge, kept the map but didn't tell anyone.

"After the war, when people were migrating and all the national rebuilding was going on, the woman moved to Kanchanaburi and left the map behind. But in 1994 she found it again when she returned to die in her home village. 75 years old, and on her deathbed, she told the story of the map to old friends who had also survived the war. News of the map's existence and of the possibility of treasure on the River Kwai created a hurricane of excitement. Treasure hunters came from all over Thailand. Even a top government cabinet member invested a lot of his own money in the search. He spent millions of Baht on big equipment and workers to dig into the mountains. It lasted for almost a year, but when no one found any treasure, the fervor slowly died down. A lot of people started claiming it was a hoax. Now only a few diehard gold seekers are still searching.

"I still don't see what this has to do with our island cave," Kevin interrupted.

Wichai looked across the table at the two Americans, "Well, last week I learned something new about this River Kwai treasure."

"So? So, what happened last week?" Kevin said.

"My grandmother lives in the village near Kanchanaburi where the old woman died last year. She and that woman were friends, and she told my grandmother before she died, that the reason no one could find the treasure was because they weren't reading the map right. There was a missing piece

The Treasure of the River Kwai

of the map that was like a key. The old woman said she didn't have the key and had never seen it. But she remembered it. After no one found any gold, she remembered that her Japanese boyfriend had told her another soldier had the key. Two Japanese soldiers were both needed to find the treasure. It was their way of protecting the gold."

David and Kevin hardly noticed as the waitress served the meal and poured more water for the three. The incredible story, parts of which were familiar to David, all of which was new to Kevin, had suddenly, through the link with this Thai friend sitting across the table, become very real. The waitress finished and left, and the boys stared at each other.

"Sounds kind of far-fetched to me," Kevin said doubtfully.

"No, it's possible, Kevin," David said. "There was a lot of confusion at the end of the war. The Japanese were suffering huge losses and the Allies were advancing on them. Conditions had gotten real bad—the River Kwai horror story was very real. I'm sure the whole looting thing wasn't a very organized operation, and probably some of the Japanese soldier units were stealing and hiding the loot on their own too."

"Hmmm . . ." Kevin said, rubbing his chin. "Question: Why did no one know there are two halves to the map?"

David shrugged. Wichai started to answer but Kevin interrupted to complete the joke.

"Answer: Because no one could read the Japanese line at the bottom of the first half that said: Tear along dotted line."

The Treasure of the River Kwai

David laughed. Wichai didn't catch the American humor. He looked at Kevin, perplexed, then continued. "I was visiting my grandmother recently and she told me about it. She says that before the old woman died she told only a few people about the key. Even most of them thought it was the fantasy of a demented old woman. And honestly, a lot of crazy stories have been floating around since it all started. But my grandmother insists that the woman was rational and serious when she told her about the key."

"So, where is the map key?" Kevin asked. Neither of the Americans had touched their food. Both leaned forward and looked at Wichai in anticipation. Kevin looked around to see if anyone in the restaurant was eavesdropping on them.

"The missing map key was carried out of Thailand by the other soldier during the Japanese withdrawal. He assumed his comrade had the other half of the map, but of course, the other soldier had entrusted it to the Thai woman. The old woman insists this is what happened: pirates in the Gulf of Thailand attacked the small troop carrier on which the first soldier was sailing and all hands were killed. The pirates robbed the boat of everything, including all the weapons, the small amount of gold and the map key, which they probably didn't really understand. They sunk the Japanese boat and hid the treasure in a cave on an island near Koh Samui."

"How would an old woman know all those details, if everyone was killed?" David asked, finding some of this too incredible to believe.

The Treasure of the River Kwai

"Because these same pirates later attacked another Japanese vessel, this time a gun boat, but failed to take the ship. I guess they figured they needed more weapons and ammo or something. Anyway, the pirates were captured, but before being executed by the Japanese right there in the Gulf, one pirate confessed the facts about his involvement in the previous attack on the personnel carrier. It seems that even in his confession all he knew was that they took some gold and stuff. I don't think the pirates knew they held a key to another map and more treasure.

"Anyway, after learning about the gold from the pirate, the Japanese kept him alive and came to Koh Samui looking for the treasure. Maybe they knew about the map key. I don't know. But, during the search among the islands they were confronted by the Allied forces that had steamed into the Gulf. The Japanese ship wasn't supposed to be there because the war was over and they were supposed to be leaving. Anyway, the pirate escaped and the Japanese fled.

"The pirate simply moved into the Surat Thani area and concealed his criminal past. There was a lot of chaos after the war so that wasn't hard to do. But eventually the story came out when he was drunk one night and bragged about treasure to friends. The word spread, as it always does when gold is involved, and back in 1952 people started looking for gold in Koh Samui. There are over 80 islands in this area, so nobody ever found anything. But eventually the woman in Kanchanaburi heard what was happening, because for a short time that

The Treasure of the River Kwai

story was in the newspapers. The woman figured the gold they were looking for must be in a chest or box along with the map key. But she was a single woman with kids and never came south to search. After a while the gold fever died down and the story was basically forgotten. So the map key and the small cache of gold has been safely hidden for 50 years, and no one knows where it is."

"Until now!" Wide-eyed, Kevin gasped, "Maybe we found the map key!"

Chapter 5
Cupcake Island

After a restless night during which each young man tossed on his bed dreaming and thinking about lost treasure and a mysterious map key, the trio greeted the morning South East Asian sun as it come into view in the east, floating out over the waters of the Gulf of Thailand. They ate a hasty breakfast and then David, Kevin and Wichai went from store to store to buy the gear they would need for their return to Anthong Park. Their inventory of supplies included several long ropes, two flashlights with plenty of extra batteries, and a day's supply of food and water. Finding the stuff they needed, especially water proof flashlights, took more time than they expected, so departure for Anthong was delayed until the afternoon. They left the bungalow,

The Treasure of the River Kwai

hiked to the Harbor Road dock, and boarded the 4:00 p.m. ferry to Koh Nua Ta Lap.

An hour later the old smoke-spewing ferry chugged along side the dock at Koh Nua Ta Lap and off-loaded its shipment of boxes, crates, and humans. The boys found the old boat-rental man, dressed as usual in nothing but a skimpy loin cloth, cleaning one of his small skiffs. He looked up and smiled. He had expected them earlier in the day, and was waiting for them. "Tahmai mah chah, khrap?" he asked with a grin. Decaying teeth glared through his red lips and gums. *Why have you come so late?* The old man spat betel-nut juice on the dock and looked at the boys curiously.

In all his years in Thailand David could not adjust to this revolting habit—chewing betel nut—favored by many village folk in Asia. The resulting red teeth and puffy gums were disgusting. David knew the nut gave a mild drug "kick." He figured they got hooked and couldn't stop. David looked at the little red-mouthed man and tried to smile. "Mee thura tee Koh Samui, khrap." David said. *We had some business on Samui Island.* The man didn't seem satisfied but shook his head and didn't ask any more questions. The boys arranged to rent the boat the next morning.

Leaving the dock area, David, Kevin and Wichai walked down the street and found the bungalow they would stay in overnight. After a meal in a small street stall, mixed with casual talk about the next day's plans, they returned to their beds and settled down under mosquito nets for a night of rest. It wasn't late, but there wasn't much to do after dark

The Treasure of the River Kwai

on these little islands. And, the previous days' discussion and sleepless night had left the three exhausted. As they drifted to sleep, each boy lay in his bed absorbed in thoughts about the next day's possibilities.

At 5:45 on Wednesday morning, the three youth, refreshed and eager to find treasure, and unable to wait any longer, left their beds and dashed to the docks. The boat rental man met them, showing obvious interest in their plans. He helped the boys load their bags and prepare for departure. Looking curiously at their stuffed bags, he asked, "Ja by ny?" *Where are you going?*

Village folk seemed to have few inhibitions about asking personal questions. In Koh Samui David had suggested they hide all their gear inside closed bags. This would help avoid too many questions. They bought an extra vinyl bag and stuffed everything in. As expected, the old man asked about the gear. Kevin pulled some Thai currency from his pocket and handed him the payment for the boat. The money worked its charm. Distracted, the old man turned away and walked barefoot up the dock counting the notes in his hand.

The boys threw their gear and food bags into the boat and jumped in. Kevin tugged vigorously on the starting rope and the old boat motor roared to life. The morning breeze felt cool in David's face as the boat pushed lazily through the water. He sat in the bow and watched the outer islands of Anthong slowly approach to the north.

The air was calm, the Gulf water flat, and except for the movement of air and water stirred by their

The Treasure of the River Kwai

boat, and the occasional squawk of a sea gull in the distance, everything around them was quiet. The boat pressed forward and David dragged his hand through the water. It felt warm. He leaned over the small side to watch the water ripple through his fingers. It was hard to see below the surface at this time of the morning, even though the water was pretty clear. The morning sun, not yet bright enough to penetrate the surface, brimmed over the watery horizon. Thai fishing boats, already at work in the bountiful waters, sat like silhouettes on the horizon, their masts and sides blackened by the glare of the morning sun.

David shadowed his eyes with his hand and squinted. "Man, these fishermen get out early!" Looking at the orange glow rising in the east, David figured it would be another two hours before the Gulf waters really showed their beautiful tropical colors.

"Gosh, what a day!" Kevin exclaimed from the back of the boat. He sat in the stern gripping the throttle. Kevin loved to drive. The little two-cycle engine whined steadily. It was too small for speed, but Kevin enjoyed the feeling of its power as the propeller pushed the skiff through the water.

Wichai reclined silently on the middle seat. "Not a cloud in sight!" Kevin said. "Man, I hope this weather holds until we get back." Clear skies were a good sign, but the boys knew that clouds and rain could come quickly in the monsoon season, and they could get soaked.

"Yeah, that would be a dud to get rained out." David said.

The Treasure of the River Kwai

Wichai turned and looked at Kevin and pointed at the motor. "Do we have enough gas to get all the way back tonight?"

"I hope so," Kevin replied. "I really didn't think too much about it, but I figure the old man must have filled it up again. We rented this boat on Monday and it got us there and back." Kevin kicked the external tank under his seat. It was heavy. "Yeah, there's plenty of gas."

They neared their little island, christened endearingly by Kevin "Cupcake Island" for its shape. Seeing the island exhilarated the boys. David wanted to jump to his feet, but he didn't, knowing that standing was foolhardy in the small boat. They neared the cliff face. Wichai clung tightly to the sides of the boat and David prepared to grab on. Kevin maneuvered the small boat to the same tree they had used for their dock once before. As they got close David stood in the bow and threw a rope around the lowest branch.

"Careful, man! You're rocking the boat!" Kevin teased David and Wichai hung on tightly to the sides. Wichai was obviously nervous. David turned and saw him hanging on.

"What's the matter, Wichai? Don't want to fall out?" David asked teasingly. Wichai nervously shook his head. He wasn't smiling.

"Don't you know how to swim, Wichai?" David asked, seeing Wichai's fear.

Normally such a direct question would have been embarrassing to Wichai. In Thai culture it was not polite to state the obvious, especially on personal things. But because they were good friends, and

The Treasure of the River Kwai

Wichai was experienced with Americans, David's frankness didn't offend him. He looked up at David and said, "No. I never got in the water much in Bangkok."

"Well, be careful then. There really isn't any reason you have to get wet anyway." David pulled one of their packs onto his back. He dragged himself up onto the rock face and began climbing. He had to clutch at small trees and rocks to avoid crashing back over the rocks into the water. Wichai followed carefully. Kevin shut off the engine, checked the tie ropes, and grabbed the remaining pack.

The heavy packs slowed the boys' progress to the top. They clung to the trunks of small bushes and trees, and pushed fingers and toes into cracks in the rock surface, and with each maneuver pulled themselves to the next level. The climb was not far, possibly 150 feet—and only the first twenty could be called a real cliff face—but it was a rock climb. When they reached the top all three were perspiring heavily.

"Man, I don't remember it being this hard two days ago," Kevin said between gasps for air.

"It wasn't. We weren't carrying all this stuff, and it wasn't as hot either," David agreed.

The three walked to a shady area under some brush near the opening of the cave, dropped their packs, and sat down. Gentle morning breezes had begun to blow and they relished the refreshing air. Each pulled a bottle of water from their packs and drank. The sun was still low in the morning sky but it was already warm, too warm. They drank lustily.

The Treasure of the River Kwai

"Don't drink all your water, man. We've got a whole day and no more water," David warned. He noticed Kevin was chugging his bottle pretty fast.

"Yeah, OK Mom!" Kevin said. "How 'bout a cookie, Wichai?" Kevin said offering Wichai some of his food stores.

"Thank you." Wichai took a cookie and munched on it.

After a few minutes Wichai stood up and looked around for the cave. David pointed toward the entrance, hidden out of view. Wichai found it behind a large boulder. The boulder was jammed two feet in front of the mouth of the cave. Only one man at a time could slide off the boulder and squeeze through the narrow space to enter the cave. Wichai lay down on his stomach on the boulder and leaned into the crevice. From this position he could see into the opening. A long, narrow passageway disappeared downward toward the center of the island turning east after about twenty feet. "Wow, how did you guys find this cave?"

"The real question is 'Why did we come to this island at all?'" Kevin said. "Well, we just liked its shape. Cupcake Island. It just looked cool from a distance and we wanted to climb it. Then, after we climbed up here we just kind of stumbled onto the opening. The way it's hidden you almost have to trip right over it to see it."

"Which is basically what you did." David laughed. He looked at Wichai and added, "Kevin fell right into that crack when he tried to jump over it. And that's when he saw the opening. Nice, huh?"

The Treasure of the River Kwai

"Yeah, the fall that made us rich and famous." Kevin joked.

"Yeah, dude. But we're not rich yet." David said. He looked at Wichai who was peering into the chasm. "You ready to crawl in, Wichai?"

Wichai raised his head and smiled, "Let's go!"

Chapter 6
Return to the Cave

With Kevin leading the way, the three crawled into the bowels of the cave. After ten feet the tunnel expanded. The boys stood on their feet and were able to walk in a stooped-over position. The passage darkened quickly. They turned on their flashlights. Kevin was in the lead, Wichai followed and David brought up the rear. The boys decided to take all their gear and food to save time, so each carried a pack. Once through the cramped entrance, they slung the heavy supplies on their backs. They figured they would eat in the cave and keep exploring all day, or until their batteries ran out.

When they arrived at the main chamber David and Kevin quickly crossed the room to the hole.

The Treasure of the River Kwai

Wichai lingered behind, enamored with the awe that every cave inspires in man. He looked around, pointing his flashlight. Wichai noticed the second passage—the one Kevin had discovered—positioned off to the left of the tunnel from which they entered. He walked over and pointed his flashlight beam into the shaft. After a few meters the passage narrowed sharply and dropped downward. He walked in as far as he could and searched the crevice. Listening carefully, he could hear the movement of water far below. Cooler air, a mysterious breeze, moved against Wichai's face as he leaned into the fissure.

"Hey Davy!" No one answered. Wichai turned toward the chamber and shouted again. "Davy! Come in here and look at this!" When no one responded, he dropped to his knees and crawled a little farther into the tunnel, but the shaft almost completely closed. Wichai pushed himself back up the passageway. He stood up and brushed off his pants. He looked into a few other corners of the large room and then walked carefully across the chamber to join his friends.

Kevin and David, planning to lower themselves into the hole to the boat below, tried to find something onto which they could tie their ropes. Kevin sat on the ledge and worked the rope.

"I can't believe we didn't think of bringing some kind of grappling hook!" Kevin tried again to wrap the rope around a protruding rock on the wall behind him. Its smooth, round shape prohibited any attempt at finding a secure hold. "We can't climb down with this!"

The Treasure of the River Kwai

"Why not use the ledge," David suggested, pointing at the rock shelf Kevin was sitting on. "I think you can get the rope around it and it'll grip OK."

"Yeah, maybe," Kevin agreed. "But it's going to be hard to climb off the ledge and grab the rope underneath. You can try it first." Kevin and David looked at each other and burst out laughing. "What a switch!" Kevin laughed. "Today I'm the coward!"

David grinned and said, "Go ahead and tie the rope around the ledge. You're already there. At least you'll have something to grab onto if you slip."

Kevin lay down on his belly, formed a lasso with the rope, and threw it around the rock protrusion. He knotted it securely. "There, good ole' Boy Scouts knot. Best Eagle in my den. That'll never come loose." Kevin dropped the 75-foot rope and it fell freely into the hole. David and Wichai's flashlight followed it down until it disappeared into blackness.

"Man, what a hole!" Wichai gasped. Wichai peered into the black round chasm and drew a deep breath. "How did you ever see anything down there?" he asked.

"I just saw it, sitting right here." Kevin grabbed his flashlight from the rock shelf and pointed it down. It took a moment for his eyes to focus. Each of the boys automatically got quiet as Kevin concentrated his light on the bottom. "See if I can find it again . . . Yeah! There it is! Same place we left it. Flamin'! Can you see this?"

Wichai and David strained their eyes but from their position could not see to the bottom. Lying on the rock ledge, Kevin moved his flashlight beam

The Treasure of the River Kwai

slowly forward to the bow of the boat. He followed it along the rocks and water passage on the bottom. The small light beam, powered by new batteries, was brighter on this day, but still faint from traveling more than seventy-five feet into the cave bowels. Kevin strained his eyes.

"It looks like there's a passage that goes over that way." Kevin pointed in a direction that crossed the chamber room from where they had entered.

Wichai, seeing where Kevin was pointing, said, "There's another tunnel back there. I heard water running in it."

"Really?!" David said, "Let's take a look."

"Yeah, man!" Kevin agreed. "Is that the passage I was looking at on Sunday? If we can find an easier way down than this, that'd be super. This thing scares even me." Kevin pulled himself away from the ledge. He carefully maneuvered around the hole. The boys walked across the chamber room to the second passageway. Inside, they peered into the narrow descending tunnel.

"Hey, feel that air!" Kevin said.

"Yes," Wichai said, and continued. "The tunnel gets real narrow way in there. You have to crawl on your belly about another ten feet."

"Quiet a second!" David said. "I want to listen for the water." The three boys held their breath and waited in silence for several moments. The cave's quietness settled over them. The clear sound of moving water, like the sound of water lapping over rocks, could be heard far below.

"Man, I'll bet this tunnel goes down to the same place!" Kevin exclaimed. "If this passage is open it'll

The Treasure of the River Kwai

be a lot easier than climbing down that crazy hole!" Kevin dropped to his knees. "Move back boys. I'm goin' in."

Kevin crawled into the narrow shaft. "Wichai, shine your light in here!" he ordered as he crept forward and down. Kevin crawled about ten feet into the narrow tunnel. His feet projected back to David and Wichai. Wichai squeezed in behind him uncomfortably. David smiled, thinking Kevin looked like a cork stuck in a bottle.

Kevin looked forward in the tight passage. The tunnel stopped abruptly in front of him but opened again to his left in a narrow, 24 inch crack. He inched forward and peaked into the crack. It widened almost immediately. He figured if he could squeeze his body around the corner and through the fissure, he could easily continue down the tunnel toward the bottom. Kevin also noticed that just past the crack the floor of the tunnel dropped four feet. Crawling through the crack he'd have to fall to the cave floor and then hang on because the path continued to slope away at a very steep angle.

"I want to get through here," Kevin said. "Come here and hold the light!" Wichai pushed in toward Kevin's legs that were pointing back at him. Wichai pressed up next to Kevin and reached an arm and flashlight into the narrow crack. Kevin squeezed his muscular frame through the opening. After a lot of pushes, kicks, and frustrated grunts he popped through and dropped to the rocks with a thud.

Kevin got to his feet and brushed himself off. After checking scratched elbows and knees Kevin

The Treasure of the River Kwai

looked back through the crack at Wichai. Wichai's curious gaze, illuminated by his glaring flashlight, filled the crack. Kidding Wichai playfully, Kevin said, "Cork man!"

Wichai looked at him, puzzled, so Kevin just said, "Very small hole. . . . Are you guys coming?"

While Wichai struggled through the crack Kevin turned and looked at the path that descended steeply beneath his feet. Holding onto the rough surface of the walls with one hand, and gripping his flashlight with the other, he negotiated each step, and slowly groped his way down the incline. Behind him Wichai got through the fissure more easily, and David, the tallest of three, followed with some difficulty.

Kevin smiled seeing David struggle. As the boys advanced downward they heard the distinct sound of water moving and gently splashing over rocks. The shape of the passage, sometimes wide, sometimes narrow, made progress uncertain and slow.

But then, without warning, the passage ended in big, black space. The boys simultaneously pointed flashlights at the space and saw that it was an opening, a large opening that seemed to swallow their flashlight's beam. Upon closer observation, they discovered that they were actually looking into a large cave room from a point high on one wall, like a box seat in a theater. Unlike theater box seats, there was no protection—the opening fell straight down into water. Kevin moved to the opening and looked down. They were about fifteen feet above the water. Loose gravel made his footing unsure and he almost slipped over the edge and

The Treasure of the River Kwai

plunged into the black lake below. He recovered his balance and shined his light into the water.

"This is it, guys! We found it!" Kevin shouted over his shoulder. He had to be careful not to make any quick moves, lest he slip and fall. He pointed his flashlight to the right and left across the shimmering black water, calculating that the boat was somewhere to his left. Straining his eyes, he shined the light toward the opposite rock wall, but he couldn't see anything.

"Whoa! What a drop off!" David and Wichai stared down the fifteen-foot drop into the black water. "Man, this isn't safe!"

"Yeah, I almost fell in," Kevin said. "Be careful. I've been looking over there but I can't see the boat yet."

"You forgot to bring your pack, ace!" David goaded. He was obviously a little upset that he had to carry an extra bag down the steep path.

"Sorry, man." Kevin took the pack and laid it at his feet. "Wichai, can you pull that twenty foot rope out of your bag? We need to rig something to get down here." Wichai found the rope and handed it to Kevin.

"Look at this," Kevin continued. "There is no way we can go anywhere down there without getting wet! Who knows what's in that water."

"Yeah, it looks kinda black and dirty," Wichai cautioned.

"I think, if we can get to the other side, we can walk along over there," Kevin said. He pointed his flashlight to the other side of the lake. It was about twenty-five feet across. As they studied the "lake"

The Treasure of the River Kwai

they realized it was simply an underground lagoon, long and narrow, supplied by the waters of the Gulf of Thailand. On such a small island no water flowed, except for the regular movement of tides.

"What are we going to do?" Kevin asked. "We didn't bring anything to keep our stuff dry. I guess we can't take it with us."

Hanging onto the rock wall, David leaned over the edge and looked down. "I think we should just leave all of our stuff here. We can take our flashlights and enough rope to get down into the water and maybe an extra rope in case we need it down there.

We'll just have to get wet and swim across."

"We should take the shovel too," Kevin said. David dug it out of his pack. It was a small garden tool, not much use for serious digging, but the boys had imagined they might have to dig.

"I can't swim," Wichai said.

"Oh man, I forgot!" David said. He thought for a moment and then continued, "Maybe you should stay here. Kevin and I will go down there and look around. We might need your help getting back up anyway."

Wichai did not like that idea at all. *They're going to leave me alone up here!* But he also realized he had no alternative. He couldn't swim the twenty-five feet across the water, and so the decision was already made. In his frustration he looked at David and muttered a common Thai resignation: "My Ben Rai." *It doesn't matter.* He switched to English and said, "You better get going. I don't know how long our batteries will last."

The Treasure of the River Kwai

Kevin and David looked around for a place to fasten the rope. After securing it to a large rock, and with Wichai's promise to make sure it stayed secure, they began climbing down. Kevin went first. He lashed his flashlight and shovel over his shoulder, and David shined a light. Kevin lowered himself down the rope with his hands, walking his feet down the cliff face. When he got to the water, he lowered himself in up to his waist and then let go of the rope. Kevin disappeared for a moment in the dark water. After a tense second he broke through the surface, and blew water from his lips. "Yuck, this water is warm! And it stinks!"

"Whadya mean, 'It stinks?'" David asked.

"I don't know! It smells bad. Yuck!" Kevin started to move away from the cliff face. "Come on, chicken!"

Suspicious of the smell, David shined his flashlight around the cave. Momentarily the light beam brushed the ceiling about fifteen feet above them. There, on the roof of the chamber above him, he saw them.

The Treasure of the River Kwai

Chapter 7
THE TREASURE CHEST

David's mouth dropped open and he gasped. His flashlight beam passed over the cave ceiling. Bats! Hundreds of them! They were crowded together in a grisly living carpet, hanging contorted upside-down.

"Look at that!" David yelled. "Bats! I mean hundreds of bats on the ceiling!" David swept his flashlight beam over the chamber ceiling, revealing the gray mass.

The ceiling seemed to be moving. David's stomach turned. He imagined the hideous creatures defecating continuously into the water below. Looking at their number, David marveled that they hadn't seen or heard the bats earlier.

"That's the smell, guys! They're pooping in the water!" David shouted. Wichai began snickering.

The Treasure of the River Kwai

David, tickled by the thought of Kevin swimming in bat dirt, giggled and burst out laughing. He stopped himself quickly, afraid the noise would frighten the rodents and make them swarm all over the boys. A rustling noise swept the room briefly and then subsided.

"We better be quiet or we'll spook them," David warned.

"Gag! Gag! Gag! Gag!" Kevin lunged and swam hard for the other side. He yanked himself out of the water onto the rocks. He rolled over and sat up, shaking in revulsion. "Yuck! Oh, man! Bat crap all over me! I can't believe it!" Kevin sat facing the water, and held his arms up like wings, not wanting to touch himself. David watched him, trying not to laugh at Kevin. David felt revulsion rise in his stomach as he realized it was his turn to climb down.

Kevin looked up at David's flashlight beam and yelled, "Come on, pal, it's your turn. Let's get this over with. This just got really unfun!"

In the glare of their flashlights, Kevin looked up at David and Wichai. His arms were still stretched out to his sides like bird wings. "Gag, this feels really awful."

"Oh well, it can't be all that bad. What's the worst that can happen—we all get hepatitis?" David said wryly. He pushed his flashlight into his pocket and started the climb down. Wichai shined the light, and tentatively turned the beam on the sleeping bats. They remained undisturbed, so far. Kevin grabbed his flashlight from his wet pack and pointed it toward David.

The Treasure of the River Kwai

Knowing what was coming, David decided to try to avoid going into the water over his head. He couldn't stand the thought of getting bat dirt in his ears and eyes. He lowered himself slowly. When he was up to his chest in the water, he released the rope. Feeling the same revolting spasms, he quickly swam across and climbed out.

"Let's go, man," David said. The two boys began walking in the direction of the boat, their enthusiasm dampened by the filthy dripping water. Wichai sat on the ledge and shined his light down on them from above. For the first time this trip he was glad he couldn't swim. He didn't like all those bats directly overhead, but he was glad he didn't have to swim in that sewer below. He smiled as he watched his companions walk along the water-edge, sopping wet and shaking their arms in revulsion. He could hear them grumbling under their breath as they stumbled through the darkness on the uneven cave floor.

After a moment they found the boat. "There it is!" Kevin shouted, running ahead of David. The boat was resting on a flat rocky area out of the water.

"Wow, man! Look at this!" Kevin gushed, bubbling with excitement at the little boat. He smoothed his hand over the rough, old wood. "This is amazing! Even the oars are in pretty good shape. I wonder if it still floats!"

"It must be at least fifty years old, if it really was used during World War Two." David said. He walked around the bow of the boat, grabbed it at the front, and tried to lift it. "Man, it's heavy! It must be made from teak wood!"

The Treasure of the River Kwai

"I still have a hard time thinking of pirates during World War Two, "Kevin said, shaking his head. He kicked the boat lightly with his foot. "How did they get this thing in here?" Kevin turned from looking at the boat and, shining his flashlight, peered farther down the lake. "It looks like the cave sort of ends right down there. There must be, or used to be, an opening to the outside over there somewhere." Kevin couldn't see any opening or light from the outside.

"Hey, I got an idea!" David said. "Turn off your flashlight." Both boys turned off their lights at the same time. The room went instantly and totally black.

"What are you doing?" Wichai's faint call whispered through cave. He had seen the flashlights go out.

Kevin turned his light on. "We're OK, man."

"Turn it back off!" David insisted. "We can look down that way and see if there is any natural light coming in. If there is, that will be the opening to the outside. Maybe we can go out that way too."

"Good idea!" Kevin switched off his light again and the boys strained into the blackness. They saw nothing. "Man, I can't see my hand two inches in front of my face!" Kevin said. "There's no light in here at all. This is creepy!"

The boys turned on their flashlights. "Yeah, looks like whatever hole used to be there is now closed." David and Kevin shined his light out over the water.

"Hey, there's the hole we looked down!" Kevin shouted. "And there's the rope we tied off! Oh, wow man! It's hanging right down into the water!"

The Treasure of the River Kwai

"Wanna try climbing up that way?" David said with a smirk.

"We might have to if we can't get back the other way. That crack was too tight, I'm telling ya. Especially for you!" Kevin swept his light around the opposite end of the cave where water and the gray rock wall met. "I wonder where the exit to the Gulf used to be over there. How else could they have gotten this boat in here?"

David was examining the inside of the boat, scanning his light on the floor of the ten-foot-long craft. "What I wonder is if there is a map in here somewhere. Or treasure." He looked more closely at the boat. It had three bench-seats, one each at stern and bow and one in the middle for the oarsmen. David looked under each but found nothing.

"I can't believe we're doing this! Hunting for treasure in some exotic cave in Thailand!" Kevin gushed. "What would my friends think back home?!" Kevin walked around the boat and shined his light on the cave wall. The boat was pulled onto a rock surface at a point where the underground rocky beach widened into a sizable room, about twenty feet deep. The ceiling above the water was high and cathedral-like, narrowing at the peak over thirty feet above them. But the ceiling over the beached boat was low and uneven, not more than ten feet high at the highest point. The boat lay in the room far enough to keep it permanently out of the water, high or low tide.

The boat was pulled out of the water, bow first, and was pointing toward the back of the chamber. David inspected the boat for clues. At the bow he

The Treasure of the River Kwai

noticed a faint arrow scratched in the flat triangular wood at the bow point. "I wonder if this arrow means anything?" It pointed straight off the bow. With his flash light beam he followed the direction of the arrow from the boat to the rocky floor. Ten feet from the bow he found another small arrow, carved permanently into the rock. "Look at this, Kevin! What is this?"

"What is what?" Kevin asked.

"It's an arrow pointing towards those rocks." David pointed his finger toward the back of the room where rocks lay in a pile. "That's two arrows pointing this way. Do you think it might be under those rocks?"

David and Kevin looked at each other in amazement wondering if their quest on this day could be so easily achieved. David began moving rocks from the pile. Kevin held the flashlight beside him. After a few minutes they exchanged jobs. Kevin used the shovel he had carried on his back. He dug at the loose dirt and small stones. Within minutes, only two feet into the pile, he hit a metal object.

"Woah, man! What was that?!!" David cried, when he heard the clang of metal against metal. He brushed stone and dirt away from the spot and uncovered the rusty corner of a steel box.

"Oh gosh, it's a treasure chest!" Kevin's eyes were round with amazement. He poked it with his shovel. "It's made of metal and wood!"

"This is incredible! I can't believe it!" David was trembling with excitement. "It's like a movie or something!"

The Treasure of the River Kwai

"Let's get it out, man!" Kevin began digging around the sides of the box and soon uncovered it enough for David to pry it loose from its fifty-year hiding place.

David placed his flashlight on the cave floor and pointed it toward the pile. He pulled at the box, and said, "Man, this thing is heavy. Give me a hand."

Kevin laid his shovel on the ground. Lifting together, the boys pulled the box free. They carried it to a smooth spot on the cave floor. The chest was about 14 by 10 by 10 inches and was made of heavy wood wrapped by wide steel bands. The lid was not hinged but was bolted down tight on two sides and secured by two locks. It was worn but seemed intact and did not look wet or rotten.

"Should we try to open it?" David asked, looking at the solid box. He grasped one of the locks and pulled at it. The metal was old and faded, but seemed tight and strong. He lifted the chest off the floor a few inches and dropped it. "Man, it is heavy!"

"I think we should just take it back up with us and open it outside where we can really see." Kevin said.

"Yeah." David turned and pointed his flashlight at the pile of rocks. "I wonder if there is anything else in there. Bring that shovel over here a minute."

With David shining his light on the rock pile Kevin dug for a few minutes but uncovered nothing else.

"What are the chances that the map key is in there?" Kevin asked, pointing at the chest. "It sure looks heavy enough to have something more than

The Treasure of the River Kwai

a map in it. Maybe gold? What's in there might be enough anyway, and forget about the River Kwai!"

David laughed, still feeling giddy with the discovery and what might be inside the chest. "Yeah, really. I guess it'd be a hassle if we carried this thing all the way out and then didn't find anything. But I don't feel like breaking it apart in here. And anyway, I think we should let Wichai help."

Kevin had forgotten about Wichai. "Yeah. I wonder how he's doing." Kevin turned and yelled toward the lake, "Hey Wichai!!! Can you hear us?" His voice echoed through the chamber.

After a moment they heard Wichai's faint voice reply, "Where are you guys?"

"We found it, man! We found it!" David shouted in Thai. "We're coming! We'll be there in a few minutes!"

Chapter 8 TREASURE!

"Let's go." David said to Kevin. "We'll open it up there." The boys picked up the box, pinched their flashlights under their arms, and began walking sideways out of the room toward the water. They had to go slowly because of the rocky edges along the water. Several times they tripped and almost dropped the chest.

"There's got to be an easier way to get this dumb box out of here." Kevin gasped. Jerking his head toward the return path, he said, "There's no way we'll be able to get it back up that way."

David looked back toward the boat and got an idea. "Put this thing down a minute." He motioned toward the rope hanging in the water and said, "Why don't we tie it to that rope and haul it up that way? If

The Treasure of the River Kwai

the boat floats we can ride it out there and get right under the hole. We won't even have to get wet! And anyway, there's no way we can swim across the water with this thing. And we shouldn't let it get wet."

"Preemo idea, man!" Kevin grinned at David. "Let's do it!" They carried the chest back to the boat and laid it on the rocks. "We better check to be sure this thing floats before we go out into the deep part. That'd be great, losing the chest in the water right after we found it."

Together they grabbed the boat and shoved it slowly into the water. Both climbed in and Kevin manned the oars while David shined the light ahead. He looked back at the chest lying on the rocks, feeling uneasy about leaving it there. He knew no one else was nearby, but David had the anxious feeling that someone might steal his treasure.

His treasure? David had grown up in a family that taught him the value of sharing and the dangers of greed. But David could feel greed, possessive and powerful, rising inside.

David checked the bottom of the boat to see how it was doing in the water. OK. No water in the boat. Good. He looked up and saw they had almost reached the rope. It rose mysteriously straight up, like a beanstalk ascending into the clouds. It disappeared into the blackness above them. Coming along side David grabbed the rope and pointed his flashlight straight up through the hole. The hole in the roof, thirty feet above them, opened like a huge chimney pipe into oblivion.

"Man, what a hole! Look at that!" Kevin craned his neck back and stared up. He couldn't see much.

The Treasure of the River Kwai

Bland grayness absorbed his light beam. He noticed that the flashlight beam was not as bright as before. "I think our batteries are wearing out."

"Yeah." David turned his attention back to the boat. "Well, the boat seems to float fine. Whadya think?" He looked over the side of the boat and checked the bottom again for water leakage.

"Looks OK. I think it'll work. Let's get the chest." Kevin shined his flashlight at the shoreline to check the box. Like David, he was worrying about possible treasure and how they would divide it among themselves. He was apprehensive about Wichai. He figured Wichai could wage an argument about the treasure belonging to the Thai people and therefore oppose any claim two Americans had on it. Kevin's stomach churned a little as he rowed the boat towards shore.

Kevin landed the boat and, after they placed the chest in the middle on the floor, they re-launched and headed back to the rope. It was only about 50 feet from the shoreline so they got there without difficulty. "Is there enough rope to tie that thing right?" Kevin asked. "We didn't bring any more rope like we said we were going to."

"Yeah, there's enough. A bunch is hanging down in the water. Here, you tie this. You're better with knots than I am." David pushed the rope to Kevin and held his light while Kevin wrapped the rope and secured the chest.

"There. That'll hold it." Kevin gave the rope a pull to be sure it was secure above them. Looking at David, he asked, "What are we gonna do now? We can't let the treasure just hang here in the water. We'll have to swim back."

The Treasure of the River Kwai

"Why don't you tie it up higher on the rope and we'll just let the chest hang above the water. We can use the boat to get back up to Wichai and then we can just pull up the treasure when we get back up to the top room."

"Yeah, that'll work." Kevin said. They grabbed the chest. David held it, clenching the flashlight in his teeth and grunting under the weight, and Kevin tied the rope. When he finished, the chest hung spinning in the air about two feet above the boat. The boys watched as the current of the water slowly drifted them away from the chest. The box slowly twisted in a circle. The rope squeaked eerily. As they rowed away both boys studied the rope and knots uneasily. They hoped it would hold until they could retrieve their treasure.

Using the oars Kevin maneuvered the boat back toward Wichai. They soon saw the dim light of his flashlight above them. Wichai saw them coming and stood up. He shined his light down into their eyes. "Is that the boat?" he asked.

"Yep. It still floats! Isn't this cool?!" Kevin yelled back.

"And we found a box near the boat!" David added. They pulled the boat into position and climbed back up the cliff. David told Wichai about their discovery and the box. The boys quickly climbed up the path. They squeezed through the crack leading back to the chamber. Their flashlights were noticeably faded when they got to the hole. The rope, still squeaking and turning slowly, stretched into the blackness. Eager to pull the chest up, but needing better light, they replaced batteries in each flashlight.

The Treasure of the River Kwai

Kevin volunteered to crawl back out on the ledge. Because of the weight and awkwardness of the box, he asked David to help him. Wichai stood across from them and shined two flashlights into the hole. Kevin lay down on the ledge and grabbed the rope. "I think I better leave this thing tied in case we drop it on the way up," he said.

"Good idea. What do you want me to do?" David was kneeling behind Kevin on the narrow ledge that skirted the hole. He kept his back against the cave wall, not wanting to lean too far forward into the hole. Vertigo affected his sight when he looked down into the murky yellow and gray glow of the hole.

"When I get this thing up high enough, grab some of the extra rope and be my safety, OK?" Kevin began pulling on the rope, grunting each time he moved it up, hand over hand. "Man, this is heavy!" He grunted a few more feet of rope and stopped, holding tight to the rope with two hands. "Can you grab that end and help me out? I'm running out of power here."

David reached, grabbed the rope, and pulled it tight. "Do you want me to give you a break?"

"If I let go the box will crash against the side of the hole and then it might snag or break loose," Kevin grunted, trying to hold on to the heavy load pulling invisibly far below. "Ugh. Hey, I got an idea." Kevin moved the rope to the other side of the pointed ledge so the rope rested on the ledge like a pulley. "Now pull it up tight and hang on!" David pulled and Kevin let go, transferring the full weight of the box to David's arms.

The Treasure of the River Kwai

"Man, this thing is heavy!" David gasped, straining on the rope and trying not to tumble off the ledge. "I can't do this for long!"

Kevin sat up and grabbed the rope again. "OK, listen. I'll pull and you just keep up the slack for me. When I need to rest a little you can hold it. Got it?"

"Yeah, ready."

"OK, here goes." Kevin heaved on the rope, bringing it up one arm's-length, then he changed hands and pulled again. David pulled up the slack, keeping tension on the rope in case Kevin slipped. In this way they slowly dragged the box up.

Wichai, still holding the flashlights, saw the box first as it slowly rose from the cavern depths. "I see it! OOOOOOeeee, it looks big!" Like David and Kevin when they first found the treasure, Wichai shuddered with giddy excitement. "What is inside?" he mumbled to himself. Wichai remembered what his grandmother had told him about her friend's stories of Japanese maps and gold. The old lady insisted the map key existed. Now it appeared she might be right. *She'll never know,* Wichai thought. *Some of this should be given to her family, since it was her secret that had led to the find. Maybe Davy and his friend won't want to share it because they found it themselves. But if it weren't for Grandmother's friend and me they'd never know it existed.*

Their muscles trembling with fatigue, Kevin and David dragged the chest up. "I'm going to pull this thing up on the ledge." Kevin said, groaning. "Pull as hard as you can while I try to yank it up. Ready. Go!"

David pulled on the rope and Kevin dragged the chest around from underneath the ledge where it

The Treasure of the River Kwai

was hanging. Wichai held his breath. His arm and leg muscles hardened in anxious silence. Kevin strained on the box, and with one final gasp he dragged it onto the ledge. Exhausted, Kevin collapsed over the box and hugged it. "I love you, baby," He panted.

After they rested for a moment, Kevin and David wrestled the chest around the ledge to the chamber floor. The three boys, hungry and thirsty from the ordeal, but mindful only of opening their treasure, collected their stuff. Together they lugged the heavy box toward the exit of the cave.

Emerging through the small entrance, sunlight rejuvenated them immediately and made their stomachs and mouths ache for food and water. The three found a shady place and, seating themselves, tore into their packs. With the treasure chest placed strategically in the middle, they gorged on water, canned tuna, bread and fruit. Wichai opened his paper box lunch, a Thai favorite of rice, soi chicken, and boiled vegetables. When they finished they turned their attention back to the chest.

"How are we going to get this thing open?" David asked looking at the locks and steel bands. "I almost hate to break it. The box itself is probably a valuable antique."

"Yeah, but face it man," Kevin said with a smirk, "the keys are long gone. And if we get someone to help us they'll want a cut of whatever's inside."

Wichai looked at the rocks above the cave opening. The highest point rose to about ten feet above them. "We could climb up there and throw it down. That would break it open."

The Treasure of the River Kwai

"Good idea, Wichai!" Kevin smiled at Wichai.

"Maybe we should take it back like this and open it later," David suggested. They discussed this option for a moment but quickly concluded that it would be difficult to conceal the large, square box. And, if the contents were not valuable, they would waste no time or effort in transporting worthless sand (as Kevin suggested might be inside) all the way back to Koh Samui.

It was agreed that Kevin and David would carry the chest to the rock summit and throw it down. Wichai remained below to watch for any of the contents that might otherwise scatter and be lost. David and Kevin quickly, but with some effort to drag and carry their treasure, reached the top of the rocks. They looked down momentarily to calculate exactly where to drop the chest. Hesitating to look at each other in gleeful, childish anticipation, they gripped the chest and counted to three. The box swung over the edge in slow motion, and fell, crashing on the rocks below. It split wide open.

Wichai, seeing the contents of the chest spill from its broken bowels, exclaimed, "OOOOOOOh, look!"

David and Kevin stood transfixed above him. A quiet pall settled over the three boys. The morning sun had nearly reached its mid-day apex on its routine trek across Thailand's tropical sky, and in this high position it cast shadows off David and Kevin, shadows that dropped over the rocks in front of them and touched the shiny stuff laying on the ground at Wichai's feet.

"We're in a lot of trouble, man!" Kevin said.

Chapter 9

THE JEWELRY STORE

Sawang Weradrasme sat on a folding chair reading the morning newspaper in front of his uncle's jewelry shop on an obscure alley in the heart of Bangkok's Silom business district. Tall apartment and office buildings shaded the narrow alley on both sides, blocking the intense morning sun, but still Sawang was perspiring heavily. He wiped his brow with a cloth and tried to concentrate on the headlines. The stifling heat and dirty air from Bangkok's traffic made his lungs hurt and eyes burn. He leaned back on his chair and tried to relax.

The local section of the paper was again carrying news about gold digging in Kanchanaburi Province near the River Kwai. Sawang smirked as

The Treasure of the River Kwai

he thought of the gullible folks throwing away their life's savings in a futile attempt to find gold that did not exist. He had his gold, right here in his uncle's store. No amount of media hype could convince him of tall tales about Japanese treasure. Still, it was entertaining.

The article included a copy of the original treasure map. Reportedly, the map had been in the possession of an old woman in a village outside Kanchanaburi, but after her death it was stolen. The first gold diggers found nothing in the jungles. The story said the map had exchanged hands several times and copies were made. Eventually the map was widely circulated. Now it seemed that copies, drawings, and "enhanced" renditions of the map were available everywhere. Sawang had seen better copies than the one he now examined. In his mind it all added up to a hoax. After more than a year of searching and digging, no one had found a single gold coin or bar in Kanchanaburi. He smiled, wiped his sweaty face again, and turned the page. It was almost ten o'clock in the morning and the shop would soon open for business. *Plenty of "gold" to be bought and sold today,* he thought. Sawang had no need for adventure in Kanchanaburi.

Sawang was twenty-nine, of slender build and handsome features. He had lived his entire life in Bangkok, growing up in a middle class neighborhood with a younger brother and sister. His family, mostly business people, owned and operated small businesses throughout Bangkok. His father and mother ran two shop house grocery stores in Din Daeng; Sawang had grown up in the apartment

The Treasure of the River Kwai

above one of them. Another uncle owned a used car and automotive repair lot. Uncle Chan owned the jewelry and gold shop in which Sawang now worked. It was the family's most profitable business, and that was his original attraction to it.

Sawang had opted out of going to college ten years before to work with his uncle and since then had done very well. He owned a car, lived alone in his own apartment that was modestly but tastefully furnished, and had enough cash to enjoy life in the fast lane in Bangkok. He wasn't wild like a lot of his friends, a good Thai/Chinese upbringing had made certain of that. But he didn't waste his evenings in front of the television either. And with Thailand's booming tourist industry, and native lust for gold, it seemed like everyone wanted to buy his country's most alluring metal. Sawang figured his profession was secure for a long time.

So it came as a real surprise on this particular morning for Sawang to be visited by a former neighbor kid and two Americans. They entered his shop talking about gold and the River Kwai. They hadn't quickly offered that information, but he twisted it from them. They asked him to buy some gold and help them sell some more, but wouldn't immediately reveal where they got it. He insisted he could not buy gold without knowing whether or not it was legitimate. This was not necessarily true, for Sawang frequently bought illicit gold when his own purposes were served. But he used the claim as leverage for information because he sensed an opportunity. He pressed the three youths for more details, convinced them to trust him, and soon got

The Treasure of the River Kwai

the entire story. It was a rousing tale of adventure and discovery in a cave near Koh Samui.

At first, the chronicle was almost too incredible to believe, but then the boys opened their shoulder bags and showed him the stash, more than 100 vintage Thai and Burmese gold coins and two half-kilogram gold bullion bars. The whole cache must have been worth over one million Baht ($25,000). He was sure the boys had no real idea the value of this cache. They wanted to sell the bar, they said, to finance their next journey to Kanchanaburi to look for more gold. Feigning ignorance, Sawang asked about their plans and offered to help. He agreed to buy the bar for 120,000 Baht ($3000), a good price for him, and the deal was made. He suggested a couple of banks they could use to secure the remainder of their treasure. He had offered to hold it for them in his shop, but sensing their hesitation and not wanting to alienate them, he directed them to a nearby bank. The three departed, cash and coin bulging from their sacks. Sawang quickly enlisted a colleague to follow them, and in this way David, Kevin, and Wichai were compromised.

Wichai went ahead to the bank to arrange a safety deposit box while David and Kevin walked to a restaurant to review their situation and make plans.

"How do you really feel about that guy?" Kevin asked as they walked toward the Bangkok Bank on Silom Road. "I'm not sure we can trust him."

"Well, I don't trust him," David said. "But what choice do we have? This is the only gold dealer Wichai knows in Bangkok, and I don't know anyone. We've

The Treasure of the River Kwai

got to sell some of this gold to get some money so we can make the next trip to Kanchanaburi. I figure we have to take some chances, and this is the first. But we've got to keep the map key a secret."

The boys had agreed that they would not, under any circumstances, tell anyone about the map key. Their fear was that outside knowledge of the map key could be an instant death sentence. Many people would kill to possess that key. And although they felt forced to tell Sawang about how they found the gold and what their plans were, they avoided revealing the existence of the map key.

They found the map key in the treasure chest with all the coins, wrapped in wax-covered paper and sewn into a leather pouch. It was in good shape for being nearly fifty years old. The map key was simply an additional, smaller map that charted a short course from the "X" on the first map. Except for a few portions of Japanese script, the map was a drawing, showing a jungle area—probably the location of the current dig—and three other distinct spots that looked to be landmarks. By visualizing a rough triangle made by the three points, one could pinpoint an accurate path to the correct hiding spot. After examining the main map and the map key the boys concluded that the treasure was located in a rocky area, possibly another cave, near the river, within a mile of the current dig.

David and Kevin walked down Silom Road to the McDonalds at Central Department Store. Over a hamburger they discussed their situation, unaware that a man was watching them across the street.

The Treasure of the River Kwai

He stood watch nearby, leaning against a pole, his arms crossed in a relaxed pose, and waited.

"We've got to make some plans to get to Kanchanaburi in the next few days," David began, "to see what we can find. Besides just doing this in a sort of 'banzai' fashion, no plans, just go and look, I don't know what else we can do. We don't know how much treasure will be there. We don't know how it's buried or hidden. Will it even be there? Really we don't know squat about this. We're flying almost totally blind."

"So, we go up there and take a look," Kevin agreed. "But we also need to talk about what we're going to do with whatever we find," Kevin said. "Are we just going to split it up three ways, or what?"

"No, we can't do that," David said. "There's no way, unless it's just small stuff. If it's a pile we'll have to think about giving a good portion to the Thai government. They'll find out anyway and we could get into big trouble. I'm sure they'll let us keep some of it for ourselves."

"Yeah," Kevin said, "But it stinks. We find it, we get it, they take it."

"The gold is the treasure of Thailand," Wichai added. "It was stolen from us by the Japanese. There is probably some gold from Burma, Malaysia and Singapore too, but the Thai government will want their gold back. They might pay a reward to whoever finds it."

"Well, I still don't like it. If they want it, they should go get it themselves," Kevin said.

"Not really, Kevin." David wasn't really sure of himself on this, but he continued. "Every country

The Treasure of the River Kwai

has treasure hunters who know what they find might be claimed by someone else. They have to defend their right to keep it. There's always a negotiation. We'll never be able to do that here. We're foreigners. The best we can do is keep some of it. But even a little will be a lot to us."

As the boys considered possibilities it was agreed that they must make an exploratory trip to Kanchanaburi. Later, depending on the outcome, they could make further plans. They figured they could go to Kanchanaburi and find the treasure within several days. Then, if the treasure was large, they would take a sampling, as much as they could carry, and return to Bangkok. There they would get some legal advice, and inform authorities. They decided to keep the Koh Samui treasure as their own, use it to finance their next journey, and divide between themselves any remainder. They figured the Koh Samui treasure was worth a lot.

As the discussion continued the boys slowly realized the seriousness and enormity of their plans. Youthful excitement gave way to sober apprehension as they realized people could kill for gold.

"I need to call Kate . . . and I think I should tell my folks," David said after they had sat in silence for a few moments.

Kevin took a long drink of his Coke, and then looked sternly at David. "Look, David. If you tell your parents what we are doing there is no way they are going to let you go. This whole thing will unravel at the seams and we'll be lucky to even keep this money. I know how you feel, but I don't feel as loyal to my folks as you seem to yours, and I'm not telling

The Treasure of the River Kwai

them. Besides, if you tell your folks it will ruin it for all of us."

David looked sternly back at Kevin, alarmed at his firmness. "I know what you're saying, but this isn't some walk in the park either, Kevin. I grew up in this country. Thailand isn't the United States. Kanchanaburi is frontier area and parts of it are pretty wild. If we just act like tourists and a Thai friend we should be OK. The Smiths can help us some to find our way around. But if we start snooping around the gold digging area we might get into trouble. I'm already nervous about that Sawang guy. Who knows what he is capable of?"

"Yeah, I know," Kevin agreed. "But Wichai said he was their neighbor and stuff."

Wichai walked up and sat down with David and Kevin. "I got a safety deposit box and put all the coins in it," Wichai said. "I had to put it in my name only because you weren't there and I'm not sure they would let a foreigner get a box anyway, unless you had all your passport and visa stuff here with you. It was no problem for me because our family uses another branch of this bank, and I showed them my account numbers. It was easy."

"Well, that's done," David added. "Look, Kevin, I've got to think about whether I tell my folks. I'm not comfortable with this at all. We've got to do the right thing here. Anyway, I need to go call Kate."

Chapter 10

KATE

Kate Smith sat up in her bed as Thailand's tropical sun rose warmly over the city of Kanchanaburi. She stretched and rubbed a short night's sleep from her eyes. Only a few weeks remained until she and her family would leave Kanchanaburi for a six-month furlough in the United States. Kate was looking forward to America. She had rarely visited "the States" in her 17 years. She'd miss her friends at Dalat School next semester, but she was eager to go "home."

Kate turned on her bed and stared out the second-floor window of her bedroom. The "Children of Hope" Orphanage children were up and playing in the yard. They lived in a house adjacent to the Smiths, on the same property. A high wall sur-

The Treasure of the River Kwai

rounded the whole place. Kate remembered when they first moved here eight years ago. That wall seemed cold and threatening. She soon discovered that almost all properties had walls like this. Now it felt normal. *"Thailand is home too."* Standing and looking out the window, Kate felt these words more than she thought them. She stretched again, and walked to her bed and sat down on the pink and yellow flowered sheets.

Funny, America didn't really feel like home. A lot of missionary kids weren't sure where "home" was. Thailand had been home since she was seven. The Smith's came to Bangkok first. Kate's parents studied the Thai language there for two years. She and her younger brother Darryl home schooled during that time. Then they moved to Kanchanaburi. They'd been in Thailand for ten years! And they hadn't been back to America for over four. It seemed like a lifetime! Anyway, Kate was excited about going "home" again for furlough. But she was also nervous about the trip.

Kate sighed and looked around her room. She had stayed up late again, watching an American movie. A romantic comedy, her favorite. Movies were a great way to get the latest in American stuff. American music was fun too. Tapes and CDs, both the legal and pirated kind, were easy to buy in Thailand; and American culture, for sale via the miracle of mass media, was popular in Thailand. Kate didn't like everything her home country represented to the world, but she wanted to be a little more familiar, so she bought CDs and rented videos to fill in the gaps about American pop

The Treasure of the River Kwai

culture. She'd heard some scary stories from other missionary kids about going home and feeling like a total outsider. This was the best way, at least right now, to plug in. Not everything about America was good—or attractive, but she was sure she could find her way around.

Kate missed her friends at Dalat. After school closed for the summer break, nearly everyone left Penang and returned to their homes all over Asia. So, here she was in Kanchanaburi. Kate didn't want to spend her whole vacation here. Except for helping around the orphanage, which she enjoyed, there wasn't much to do, so she was glad to go to America this year. Bangkok, on the other hand, was fun. Lots of shopping, activities and friends. Some of her friends lived in Bangkok, so she hoped to see them before they left Thailand. The Smith's planned to spend a few days in Bangkok before departure.

Kate got out of bed and stretched. She walked to the mirror over her bedroom vanity and stared disapprovingly at her reflection. Her long, brown hair, tousled from sleep, hung loose on her shoulders. Kate was average height and build for her age. Her brown hair was accented by striking brown eyes, a quality frequently noticed by teenage boys. She frowned into the mirror and tried to tame her hair with her fingers.

Kate wasn't angry about her situation. She respected her parents and their work. Sufficiently mature for her seventeen years, she realized her parent's presence in Thailand had merit. The orphanage work was helping a lot of children, some

The Treasure of the River Kwai

of whom Kate had grown up with. And, they *were* going back to the U.S.—at least to visit. "But I don't want to be here forever!" she said to her reflection in the mirror.

Her mother yelled up the stairs, interrupting Kate's day-dreaming, "Kate! KATE! Are you up?!"

"Yes, Mother! I'm getting dressed."

"David Carson is calling from Bangkok!"

Kate ran to her door, pulled a light bathrobe over her night clothes, and tying it quickly at the waist, bounced down the stairs. She grabbed the phone from her mother. "David! Hi!"

"Hi, Kate. How are you?" David's voice crackled over the line.

"I'm . . . I'm great. I just got up. What time is it?" Kate looked around for the kitchen clock. Kate felt a little dizzy. David Carson had that effect on her.

"I'm sorry, Kate. I guess it IS early. I should have waited until 8 O'clock."

"No, no! That's fine. I was already up. I was just wondering . . . I mean I was glad to . . . Uh . . . Anyway, where are you?" She was really falling all over herself. G*eez.*

"Kevin Merritt and I are in Bangkok. We've just come up from Kevin's house in Surat. We're thinking of taking a bus over to Kanchanaburi for a few days . . . and . . . uh, wondered if you're going to be home." Now it was David's turn to feel awkward. He too had feelings for Kate, but they weren't allowed to date at Dalat, and the two had never really talked, except during group activities.

The "no dating" restriction felt like a dumb rule to David. He figured the school administrators were

The Treasure of the River Kwai

trying to please strict parents. David wasn't a rebel, but he was a young man. *It really is a good rule, I guess.* His youthful interest in girls didn't like the restriction, but his respect for his parents and the school administrators held him in line. *Limit the students, and the parents will be happy. Oh, well...*

David had known Kate and her family for almost ten years, the entire time they lived in Thailand. They had frequently been together when they all lived in Bangkok when he and Kate were kids. Their families came from the same mission. Times had changed. Now, with every encounter, there was magic in the air.

"Yeah, I'll be here for at least two more weeks." Kate said into the receiver. "We're going to the States for furlough in early August. But I'm here 'til then, except for a few days in Bangkok before we leave. When are you coming? . . . And where are you gonna stay?"

"We're not sure," David said. "We want to do some exploring in the area. Visit the River Kwai Bridge. Stuff like that. You could come along if you want." Kevin, who was standing behind David in the guesthouse lobby where they were using the telephone, poked David hard in the ribs. David turned to see Kevin frowning and shaking his head vigorously. *Whoops.*

"Sounds like fun," Kate said. "I've been bored to death this past month since school left out. There's nothing to do here, and I'm alone with my folks and Darryl. So, yeah, come on over," Kate offered again. Still blundering, she continued, "It'll be great to see

The Treasure of the River Kwai

you . . . Uh, what have been doin' since school got out?"

"Kevin and I just came from Anthong Marine Park near Koh Samui. I went down from Bangkok and we've been hanging together exploring around the islands."

"Wow," Kate gushed. "Sounds like fun!"

"Oh, man. We've been having a blast. I'll tell you all about it when we get . . ."

Kevin poked David again and hissed, "Would you shut up, David!"

David elbowed Kevin, turned sheepishly back to the phone, and said, "Listen, Kate, I've got to go. I'll call you when we get to the bus station in Kanchanaburi. We'll come by your house for a little while and we can talk more. Will that be OK?"

"That'd be fine. Please come over. Do you want me and my Dad to pick you up at the bus station? You don't know your way around town." Kate hoped he'd say yes. *Maybe my folks will invite the guys to stay in our guest room.* "I'll ask my folks if you can stay with us."

"OK. Thanks. That'd be great. I'll see you when we get there. Bye." David hung up the phone and turned to Kevin. "Sorry, man. It was out before I even thought."

"Right. Talk to Kate, lose your brain. Now we'll have four more people to divide the loot with—Kate and her family. Man! Why don't you just put it in the newspaper!?" Kevin was mad. He stared at David. "This was supposed to be our secret."

"Sorry. Kate sort of does that to me." David confessed.

The Treasure of the River Kwai

"Geez, David." Kevin mused. "Between your pining away one minute and losing your head the next, Kate pretty much takes over your brain. I almost think we should scratch the whole idea of going over there."

"I can't go to Kanchanaburi without seeing her, Kevin," David said. "Treasure or no, I've got to at least stop in and say 'Hi.' It's not just because I like her. We've been friends since we were kids. And besides, you'll want to say hi to Darryl and all. *And* it'll be much easier for us to have a contact in town if we need anything. I promise I'll be good."

"And keep your head screwed on," Kevin added. Kevin admitted to himself that it would be good to see Darryl too. Darryl was two years younger, but they were friends. *Darryl sure helped Dalat's soccer team win this year.* Darryl was the best goalie Kevin ever saw. He basically made up 90% of Dalat's defense. Yeah, for a freshman, Darryl was all right. A little weird, but all right.

David and Kevin were still sitting in the corner restaurant when Wichai returned with their bus tickets to Kanchanaburi. "Three seats on the air conditioned bus tomorrow morning, Thursday at 9:00 a.m.," he said, staring at the tickets. "It should take about two hours to get there."

For the moment, David and Kevin resolved to forget their dispute over Kate. It was decided that they should spend the remainder of the day in Bangkok buying all the supplies they'd need for their expedition. It seemed more prudent to buy supplies anonymously in Bangkok than to be seen

The Treasure of the River Kwai

buying such things in a small—gold fever—town like Kanchanaburi.

They planned to spend no more than four days in the province. If they could not locate the exact position of the treasure in that amount of time, they'd return to Bangkok and make a new plan. David's parents were willing to give the boys permission to go to Kanchanaburi to visit Kate and explore around the River Kwai Bridge, but anything more than four days seemed excessive.

David, against his own better judgment, had bowed to pressure from Kevin to not tell his parents some important facts about their real plans. Guilt for this deception gnawed at David. He wondered how long he could keep up the charade. He had told them about their discovery in Anthong, and of their plans to go exploring in Kanchanaburi Province, but kept the details vague.

The boys speculated about how difficult it would be to actually recover the gold. The newspapers had carried stories for a year about expensive digging with heavy equipment. Wealthy Thai businessmen had spent millions of Baht on the search. Caves were blown to bits, deep holes were carved into the earth, and the mountainous jungle landscape was virtually scraped clean in a quarter-square-mile area north east of the River Kwai Bridge.

Granted, everyone was digging in the wrong place. But the boys figured the Japanese could have hidden the treasure deep in the ground, or under water, or something. Even with the complete map the treasure might be hard to get out. They

The Treasure of the River Kwai

figured their only hope of recovering the treasure depended on a number of important factors. First, their map key had to be real and accurate. Second, no one else could venture into the area and discover their secret (the boys were correct when they figured that, as foreigners—even with Wichai traveling with them—they would never be allowed to keep the treasure if they were caught). And finally, and most ominous of all, the treasure couldn't be buried under a ton of rock or dirt. They hoped it was simply stashed conveniently in some hidden cave.

Common sense demanded they buy supplies for cave and water exploration. This they did, expanding greatly on the infantile excursion of Cupcake Island. To avoid drawing attention to themselves with too much luggage, they decided to reduce their clothing and personal stuff to three simple outfits each—suitable for jungles and caves—and a few toiletries. They'd use the large suitcases to pack ropes, flashlights, batteries, chemical light sticks, food, two collapsible military-style shovels, and other miscellaneous items.

The suitcases could serve a second purpose. If they found anything, they could throw the equipment away and pack the suitcases with gold. Even if they couldn't carry it all, they'd have enough to make the trip profitable. They could then notify the Thai government to go and recover the remainder.

The boys' plans quickly took shape, and while they all agreed on the basics of their strategy, each knew they were embarking on a dangerous

The Treasure of the River Kwai

mission that was potentially laden with unexpected problems. Unknown to them, this is exactly what was developing in another part of Bangkok.

Chapter 11

CONSPIRACY!

Somsuk and Kauwee jumped on a Bangkok "Tuk-Tuk" and instructed the driver to head for Din Daeng. The three-wheeled taxi, its motorcycle engine whirring like a chain saw, sped down Bangkok's busy thoroughfares and carved its way through traffic. After a grueling 30-minute ride, in which the two passengers were battered mercilessly, and were slowly covered in a grimy mixture of sweat and dirty air, the driver squealed to a stop in front of Sawang Weradrasme's jewelry shop. Thap was waiting for them.

Fate must still be smiling on me, Somsuk thought to himself. The evening before, when he met his old acquaintance in a familiar Bangkok bar, Thap told Somsuk and Kauwee a story about two foreigners who came to his bosses' jewelry store weighted down

The Treasure of the River Kwai

with gold. They sold only part of it, Thap said—a gold bar that his boss bought—for 100,000 Baht. It was worth much more, but the foreigners didn't know. After the deal, Sawang had Thap follow them. By the end of the second day he knew their plans. Thap needed Somsuk and Kauwee to make their plan work, he said, and could they meet him the next morning.

So, as the Tuk-Tuk pulled up to the jewelry shop, Thap jumped off the curb and crammed into the Tuk-Tuk with Somsuk and Kauwee. "Take us to the Dusit Hotel," Thap ordered the driver. There wasn't much room in the little open-air taxi, especially when Kauwee's ample size took half of the small seat. The taxi driver frowned and maneuvered his overburdened fare back into traffic.

Arriving at the Dusit Hotel, Thap and his companions chose a booth in the restaurant. When they were seated, Thap and Somsuk on one side, and Kauwee (the "Fat One" to use Thap's words) on the other, Thap laid out his proposition: "The foreigners are going to Kanchanaburi to hunt for the gold at the River Kwai Bridge. I think they have some extra information that they think will lead them to the gold. Anyway, they probably already have another 50,000 Baht in gold coins, besides the money they got from Sawang."

"So, what are we going to do?" Kauwee asked, slurping Thai coffee and stuffing a pastry between his swollen lips. "We need some of that. . . ."

"Shut up, Kauwee!" Somsuk kicked his stupid friend's foot, and then turned graciously to Thap. "Why are you telling us? Why don't you and Sawang

The Treasure of the River Kwai

just go and take the gold and the money from the foreigners? They're not going to do anything. They're just stupid, young foreigners. Where could they get that kind of gold?"

"I think they found it." Thap interrupted.

"Is that what they told you?!" Somsuk said. "My friend, I'm sure they didn't find it. They are stupid foreigners. If they cannot use a more creative story than that, this job will be easy. The gold must be unregistered, and who knows where those coins came from. They probably robbed some wealthy man in a village. What legal claim do they have on it? It would be easy to take it from them. They will never report it."

"I'm sure Sawang would agree with you." Thap said, looking around the restaurant nervously. "But, I overheard them talking about some kind of map that will lead them to the gold in Kanchanaburi. This is the real reason Sawang wants you. It may be a hoax, in which case just taking what those boys have already will be enough payment. But, if they really do have some special information, we could be rich! But we cannot do this job alone. My boss has a reputation for being a law-abiding citizen in Din Daeng. He really cannot involve himself in this business."

"This is very wise of him," Somsuk replied.

"So, Sawang asked me to find a few trusted friends to help me with the job," Thap continued. "You two came to Bangkok at just the right time. You must go to Kanchanaburi and follow the Americans to find out what they are doing. If they find gold, or if they will lead you to it, fate will smile on us for the rest of our lives. Either way, we will profit from the effort."

The Treasure of the River Kwai

"What arrangements are you suggesting, then?" Somsuk wanted to know what his cut would be before going any further.

Thap shifted his small body nervously in his seat, sat up straight, lifted his chin and said, "Sawang says for your work he will give you 20% of the value of the cash and gold—what they have now and whatever you find."

"What!" Somsuk snapped. "We put our necks in the sling for 20 percent!" Somsuk, in good Asian fashion, showed shock, not the outrage he really felt. *Sawang is a stinking thief!* Somsuk returned to his gracious smile. "Apparently Mr. Weradrasme thinks this job to be an easy one for us. I thank him for his confidence in our abilities. But the job will be more difficult. 20 percent is not adequate compensation."

"How much will 20 percent be?" Kauwee blurted out between gulps on coffee and pastry. "It might be enough." Pastry icing clung to one corner of Kauwee's mouth. He chewed hungrily on his food.

Somsuk frowned at Kauwee. For the first time he felt contempt for his obnoxious partner. "Let me handle this Kauwee," he muttered, then turned back to Thap. "Kauwee is my able partner, but he is not experienced in financial matters . . . We should divide the total value evenly—50 percent each. Sawang finds the job. We do the job. Even split."

"This is not possible." Thap replied, shaking his head. *What kind of idiot does this fool Somsuk take me for.* "First, there will be great risk to my boss when he sells the gold. Remember, it is unregistered," Thap explained. "Sawang will buy everything when you bring it to us. You have a guaranteed buyer,

The Treasure of the River Kwai

which makes your job much easier. Secondly, if you were to find a large cache of gold, we will find other men to help you haul it out. Therefore, this percentage is more than fair."

"I will settle for 60-40. We too are taking a great risk." Somsuk looked around the restaurant and then leaned forward across the table. Lowering his voice to a whisper, he said, "What if we have to dispose of these foreigners? Who is doing the hard work then?" He sat back in his seat and continued. "No matter what we do, I am risking the welfare of myself and my gifted partner here to do you this favor. 60-40."

Somsuk knew he was asking too much. Without the fencing assistance of Sawang, even if he and Kauwee succeeded in getting any gold, he couldn't sell it. He bluffed. "Please tell Mr. Weradrasme that I hope he can find someone suitable for this job." Somsuk rose to leave. Kauwee, still eating, looked at him with bewilderment.

Thap knew what his boss would allow, and what would be the outcome to him if he failed. "Somsuk, my friend! Please! My boss will have my head, but I will make one final offer. 70-30. I promise you I cannot do any better." It was the truth. Thap was sweating, and Somsuk could see the beads of perspiration on his forehead. He knew this was the best offer he'd get. The two negotiators, sitting side by side, stared at each other. Kauwee sat across the table eating, and paused in the silence to look at the men.

"The deal is unsatisfactory," Somsuk said, breaking the silence, "but as a favor to your boss, we'll agree to these terms."

The Treasure of the River Kwai

"Excellent." Thap looked relieved. "Upon delivery of the gold, and whatever else you may find, we will pay you 30% of the agreed value in cash." Thap folded his hands into a wai and bowed before his business opponent. Somsuk returned the favor, and with this formality the deal with set. Even in crime, certain protocol was to be followed. Now there was no turning back. They must get the gold, even if by murder. The alternative—death for crossing or failing the mafia—was too severe. "Now, you must hurry to Kanchanaburi today because the foreigners, and their Thai friend, have bought bus tickets and will arrive tomorrow at about noon. I assume they will go to the River Kwai dig site sometime tomorrow afternoon or Friday. You must arrive there before they do and wait for them. Go tonight if necessary."

Thap continued by describing the appearance of the three boys, and giving his best pronunciation of their names. He had only heard the name of Kevin (which he pronounced *Keewin*) and Wichai. He did not know the name of the other, taller youth with the blond hair.

"Fate is a mysterious thing, Kauwee," Somsuk reflected as they sat in their hotel room later that evening. "We came to Bangkok to find a way out of our trouble, and we leave with the promise of more wealth than we could ever imagine. Tonight we return to Kanchanaburi and the River Kwai to find the foreigners."

Kauwee, stuffing himself with rice and curry and guzzling a bottle of beer, shook his head in agreement.

Chapter 12

KEVIN'S BETRAYAL

David saw her when he stepped off the bus onto the street in downtown Kanchanaburi. Kate was leaning against the front fender of her dad's four-door pickup, scanning the buses that had parked helter-skelter on the street. She was wearing blue shorts and a white cotton pull-over top. She had seen the Bangkok bus arrive and, shading her eyes with her hands from the bright tropical sun, scanned the busy street. Kate completed her scan, and her eyes met David's. She ran over to him, waving enthusiastically.

"David! Hi, David!" Kate gave David a hug. They had not seen each other for more than a month and both were glad for this reunion.

"How are you, Kate?! It's good to see you!" The two gazed at each other for a moment, and David

The Treasure of the River Kwai

thought *Geez, Kate, I missed you more than I thought.*

Wichai and Kevin followed David off the bus, and Kevin crowded in to say hi. "Hey, Kate! What's up, girl?"

Kate turned to Kevin with a smile. "Hi, Kevin! So, you guys are planning some big adventure, or what?"

"Yeah, sort of." David hesitated for a moment. "Kate, this is Wichai, my friend from Bangkok."

"Sawatdee Khrap," Wichai folded his hands in the traditional wai and greeted Kate.

"Sawatdee Ka," Kate replied, using the feminine greeting. "Yindee pop koon, ka." *I'm glad to meet you.*

Wichai, pleased to meet another foreigner who could speak his language, smiled broadly. He and Kate exchanged pleasantries and Wichai complimented Kate on her fluency in Thai.

John Smith, Kate's dad, joined the group and he and the boys dragged their suitcases out of the bus storage compartments. "Looks like you guys are going on a trip," John said.

"Oh, we brought some extra stuff along. I guess we travel heavy. We want to do some hiking and exploring around the River Kwai Bridge," Kevin replied.

"Do you know . . . What is happening with the gold digging thing near the bridge?" David asked Mr. Smith. David hadn't read anything in the newspapers for a while and wondered about the latest news.

"Oh, it's sort of quieted down lately. A month ago things got pretty feverish again, when they thought

The Treasure of the River Kwai

they had found a new possible hiding place, but I don't think it ever amounted to anything. They move equipment and dig for a while. Not much is being said right now." John Smith looked curiously at the boys. "You guys going searching for gold?"

"Oh, we thought it'd be fun to look around at the dig. Kevin's never seen the River Kwai Bridge either," David said. He didn't think he was going to be able to evade the truth about their plans, and was uncomfortable with the deception. *If Mr. Smith presses us, there's no way I can avoid telling the story.* "Anyway, we're ready to do whatever."

"Sounds fun." John Smith looked at his daughter. "I suppose you are going to want to tag along on this escapade, too?"

"Can I, Dad?" Kate begged. "It'll be my last chance to hang out with David and Kevin before we leave."

"Well, I'm sure we can work something out. Let's get this stuff loaded up and we'll talk about it at home."

The boys and John Smith threw all the bags in the back of the truck and everyone piled in. They drove south through the city and within a few minutes arrived at the Smith home. Their house was located near the edge of town, in a compound that also provided housing for the 30 children in the "Hope of Thailand" orphanage. A third multi-purpose building served as housing for staff, kitchen facilities, and "family" rooms where the children could play. Sandy Smith, John's wife, emerged from this building as the truck pulled into the gravel drive of the compound. She waved and smiled.

The Treasure of the River Kwai

"Well, David Carson, how long has it been?" Sandy said with a smile. "I think you get taller every time I see you . . . and your hair is blonder too. What did you do, bleach it?" Sandy gave David a hug and teasingly tousled his hair. Sandy was a pretty woman, and always had something cheerful to say. Every time David saw Kate's mother he was reminded why he liked Kate.

"Hi, Mrs. Smith," David sheepishly combed down his hair with his hand. "I guess the sun is bleaching it. Kevin and I have been outside a lot lately."

Sandy looked at David. She had to look up a little. "So, how are your parents?"

"They're fine. I just got home about a month ago and haven't been there much. I've been down in Surat with Kevin the last week or so . . . but they're doing fine, thanks."

"So, you must be Kevin?" Sandy asked, turning to offer her hand. "I'm Sandy."

"Yes, ma'am, glad to meet you." Kevin said. "I play soccer with your son Darryl at Dalat. Is he here?"

"Yes, he's in the house. So, you know Darryl? Well, he loves soccer."

"He sure does. I'm actually a junior but we played on the same team. Dalat's not big enough to have a Varsity and Junior Varsity team, so they put us together, but Darryl's good enough for high school anyway." Kevin shifted awkwardly on his feet. The Smiths seemed real nice, he thought.

"I think he's up in his room," Sandy replied. "When we get inside I'll make sure he comes down." Sandy turned to Wichai and said, "So, David, who else is with you?"

The Treasure of the River Kwai

"This is Wichai," David replied. "We sort of grew up together in Bangkok. He studies at Ramkhanheang University in Bangkok. But he's out for break right now and we're out doing some stuff together."

"Sawatdee, ka. Pohm chu Koon Sandy." *Hello. My name is Sandy.* Sandy greeted Wichai in Thai, using the formal title *koon* in front of her name, in deference to the Thai custom of politeness when two people first meet.

"Sabai dee, Khrap. Pohm chu Wichai." Wichai replied. *"I'm fine, thank you. My name is Wichai."* Wichai did not use the formality, recognizing Sandy's seniority as an older adult. The two briefly continued a friendly exchange in Thai and then Sandy turned to the three teenagers and said in English,

"Well, you guys must be hungry after your trip. Come on in and we'll get some lunch for you. Are you planning to stay with us?" Sandy asked, leading the way into the house. Observing Thai custom, even in this American home, everyone kicked off their shoes as they entered the house. David and Kevin had to sit down on the steps to remove their sneakers.

They looked at each other briefly and then Kevin said, "Thanks, but we may try to stay closer to the River Kwai Bridge. That way we can get an early start in the morning. Maybe you could give us a lift over there today?"

"I don't know, Kevin. It might be better to stay here, don't you think?" David looked at Kevin as they entered the house and Kevin shook his head and silently mouthed the word *NO!*

The Treasure of the River Kwai

"Well, you can talk about it and let me know. We'd be glad to have you," Sandy added. "I'll check to see when lunch will be ready." She disappeared into the kitchen as the young people gathered in the living room.

John followed them in and explained that he had some things to do in the office. "I'll talk to you later, over lunch." John said. "Let me know if you want to stay and we'll bring in your things." He left the house and walked across the compound to the orphanage.

Kevin was not happy with this arrangement. Their plan was being unraveled by the involvement of too many people he didn't know. They seemed like nice people, but this wasn't the way he thought things should be working. He sat in stony silence and fumed. David could see Kevin's frustration, but felt that, as guests of the Smiths, and the fact that this family had been friends with them for a long time, he couldn't just walk away from this visit, gold or no.

The four teenagers sat on ratton furniture in the Smith's modest living room and made small talk for a few minutes. A ceiling fan overhead helped cool the tepid air in the room. Their conversation was interrupted when Darryl came bounding down the stairs. "Hey, guys! What's up?" Kevin noticed that Darryl hadn't changed much. *Still a little too pudgy around the middle*, he thought. Darryl wore thick glasses. His hair hung over his ears and a little with a "cow-lick" stuck up out of his bangs in the front—a little too long and never quite combed. *Some things never change. With his glasses and*

The Treasure of the River Kwai

that long hair, how does he see to play goalie? Kevin thought.

"Hey Kevin!" Darryl said, walking over to Kevin punching him on the shoulder. "Watcha doin' here?"

"How are you, Darryl? Playing any soccer?"

"Naw. Wish I could. I'm not here long enough to join any team, and I don't really know enough kids to do anything anyway. . . . Did you know we're going to America in a few weeks?" Darryl was excited about that.

"Yeah, Kate told us. Sounds like fun." Kevin tried to smile at Darryl. Right now, Kevin wished he could go to America. That is, right after he got his share of the gold.

"So, what are you doing here?" Darryl plopped himself on the floor in the middle of the room and pushed his glasses up on his nose. "You wanna go outside and kick some balls at me?"

"No, we're not staying too long. We've got some things to do," Kevin was getting angrier by the minute. Just being here was making it impossible to keep their plans secret. *Everybody in the world is going to know by tomorrow!*

David and Kate exchanged small talk on the sofa. Wichai was looking through some English magazines that he found on the coffee table. Kevin looked around the room. He sighed, "Yeah, I think we got time for a few good kicks!" he almost yelled at Darryl. "You have a ball?"

Kevin and Darryl jumped up and went outside. Kevin needed to kick something or he was going

The Treasure of the River Kwai

to burst. He was anxious to get going, and getting mad at David. He was tired of David leading the way and making wrong decisions. This wasn't going the way Kevin had envisioned, and it seemed to be getting worse by the minute. Darryl ran to find his soccer ball. Kevin went out into the yard and waited, fuming. *I guess I could just go it alone.* The idea was tempting, but because he didn't know the Thai language, he would be seriously handicapped to get around alone.

The two boys were soon engaged in a frenzied goal-kick duo. After ten minutes of aggressive kicking by Kevin, and zero scores because of Darryl's effective blocking technique, they quit, exhausted. They walked to the shaded porch of the house and sat down. Darryl ran to the kitchen and asked the Thai house girl to bring them some lemonade. The two sipped their drinks on the porch and cooled themselves.

"Do you speak Thai?" Kevin asked Darryl.

"Yeah, sort of," Darryl said. "I never went to language school like my folks, but I hang out with the neighbor kids and some Thai friends at church when I'm home. So I picked up a bunch of stuff I guess." Darryl tossed the ball in the air and spun it on his finger.

"I can't speak any at all," Kevin mused. "It's sort of frustrating being so dependent on these other guys. They both speak Thai and don't really need me."

"What are you doing here?" Darryl wondered. "I heard you say something about going exploring over at the River Kwai Bridge."

The Treasure of the River Kwai

"Yeah, we want to do that, and maybe check out the gold digging area just for fun. I've never seen a real treasure hunt before."

"Maybe we could go over there this afternoon," Darryl offered. "I probably could go with you and help. My folks won't let me go alone, but I could go with you."

Kevin looked at Darryl and pondered the idea. The idea of going today wouldn't work because it would raise too many questions. But he and Darryl could break from the group tomorrow and do their own search. *Maybe Darryl could help.*

"Tell you what," Kevin began. "We'll go with the others tomorrow, but you and I can split off from them and go exploring on our own. The group's too big anyway, and we can make better time on our own."

"Maybe we could go into town today and get some stuff we'll need." Darryl suggested. The two boys talked about the supplies that they might need for exploring the area. Kevin told Darryl what they had brought from Bangkok, and, showing unusual insight, Darryl offered a few suggestions about additional items that would make their search easier and more prepared.

"We can take the little motorbike. I do it all the time." Darryl offered when Kevin asked how they could get back into town without everyone else wanting to come along. Darryl ran into the house and, avoiding contact with David, Wichai and Kate, cleared the plan with his mom. Sandy wondered about lunch but Darryl said they could just pick up something in town. While he did this Kevin went

The Treasure of the River Kwai

to the truck and got his backpack. He emptied the contents into his other bag, took out the map key and made a quick copy of the drawing. He didn't want to take the original because then David would know what they were doing. He looked carefully at the drawing and quickly tried to make a rough duplicate. He stuffed this into his empty backpack and zipped it up just as Darryl came around the house riding the little motorbike. "You ready?" Darryl said eagerly. "Hop on."

Chapter 13

FOLLOWED!

Somsuk watched from a street corner as Kevin and Darryl left the orphanage compound on Darryl's motorbike. The description of the two foreigners, provided by Thap, did not fit the appearance of these two, but he never could tell one foreigner from another. He figured Thap had the same problem. *They all look alike: unhealthy pale skin and colorless hair.* The taller one must be *Keewin*, he figured. But the shorter one didn't fit Thap's description very well. Somsuk couldn't remember Thap saying anything about the kid wearing eye-glasses. *Maybe this is some other kid.* When the boys passed him—he was leaning casually on an electric pole—he looked away to avoid eye contact, but, as soon as they were down

The Treasure of the River Kwai

the street a ways, he mounted his motorcycle and followed them.

For an hour Somsuk followed the boys from one store to the next and observed as they bought miscellaneous gear and food. He tried to make sense of their purchases but eventually concluded that they were novices to the area and were simply stocking obvious supplies for a trip into the mountains. They didn't spend a lot of money and that perplexed Somsuk, because, according to Thap, they had lots of money from the sale of the gold.

After an hour, and when it became obvious the boys were heading home, Somsuk decided to leave following them and return to his house where Kauwee was probably eating or sleeping. The two men planned to rise early the next morning, probably before 3:00 a.m., to go to the gold camp and await the boys' arrival.

Somsuk followed the two boys until they turned into the gravel drive of the orphanage. As expected, Kauwee was eating when Somsuk arrived, and drinking himself drunk. "What are you doing!!?" Somsuk scolded. He stood over Kauwee, disgusted. "Drunk again! We hike into the mountains in a few hours!" Somsuk grabbed the bottle from the table. "No more whiskey!" He took a long drink from it, and cursed Kauwee. The fat man sat gravely in a wooden chair, the back creaking under his massive weight. Kauwee's oversized belly bulged out from a gap between his trousers and t-shirt. "How are you going to hike in the jungle tomorrow, Kauwee!? You'll die of sunstroke or a heart attack before we walk 10 meters!"

The Treasure of the River Kwai

"I'm scared," Kauwee confessed. "We could get killed."

"It'll never happen you idiot! I just spent three hours watching the foreigners," Somsuk said. "They're kids. We have nothing to fear. We just follow them. We can seize them at any moment, and take the map, or make them lead us to the treasure. It'll be easy." Kauwee slumped in his chair in a stupor. Somsuk continued, "The extra money, I'm not sure about yet, because they're staying. . . . Are you listening to me!? . . ." Somsuk wanted to kick his slob partner, who seemed almost oblivious to Somsuk's presence. "They're staying in a Christian orphanage compound south of here. If they leave the money there we can't get to it because lots of people live there."

Somsuk continued laying out their plans, occasionally provoking Kauwee back to reality with a curse or thump on the head. Kauwee tried in vain to concentrate. All he could think about was a difficult hike in the mountains, through hot, insect-infested jungles. This was not turning out like he had thought. Somsuk finally gave up the one-sided conversation and the two went to bed and slept fitfully.

At 3:00 a.m. they awoke and, after a few preparations and constant protests from Kauwee, were on their way. Somsuk had arranged for a friend to pick them up in his truck. He told the driver only that they had a contact to make—the man was a part of the drug world, so no other explanation was needed. The truck dropped them at the foot of the hills just past the River Kwai Bridge. Somsuk led

The Treasure of the River Kwai

the way, and Kauwee, still reeling from the drinking binge the night before, followed as they hiked up the rough road. Thickening jungles crowded both sides of the dirt road. As expected, within ten minutes Kauwee was complaining and dragging behind.

"It's only a about 2 kilometers, Kauwee. Just shut up." Somsuk barked. He was not in the mood to deal with an inferior partner. "I'm about ready to send you back and do this on my own, you slob!"

"So, I'm a slob!" Kauwee retorted between puffs for air, "But you need me. You can't kidnap those kids by yourself. No way."

The two struggled on, and after numerous stops for rest, with Somsuk cursing and yelling while Kauwee complained about the difficulty, they eventually arrived at the dig site.

The site was huge. Near a dozen large camps were distinguishable, with numerous smaller outfits struggling for space between them. One treasure hunter or his team controlled each camp, Somsuk figured. Many of the camps appeared, in this early hour, to be deserted. A few oil and kerosene lamps hung precariously on bent wooden poles outside dirty tents, glowing dimly in the morning light. A couple of camps had heavy equipment, large-wheeled trucks and earth movers, parked nearby. There was an old bulldozer covered in brown dirt, and a large crane shovel. Most of the camps looked barely functional, like they were operating with little or no money—poor souls who had scraped together meager tools and supplies in the thin hope of discovering quick riches.

The Treasure of the River Kwai

"What do we do now?" Kauwee asked, puffing and exhausted from the hike. "I'm hungry." He looked around as if to find some place to buy food.
"There's no food or restaurants for us here, Kauwee. Forget it." Somsuk glared at his partner. "We sit and wait. They will come here first. Whatever map secret they have, it must begin near here." The mismatched partners in crime sat down on an old log to wait.
Clothed in morning mist, the tropical sun slowly brimmed the hills of Kanchanaburi and cast a hazy orange glow over the River Kwai camp. At the Smith residence, Kevin and Darryl stirred from their beds, and quietly gathered their gear. The night before, Kevin, frustrated with David and the turn of events, had enlisted Darryl to join him and leave early. Kevin scribbled a quick note to David and laid it on the Smith's kitchen table—*"Couldn't sleep. Darryl and I left early to get started. Will meet you at the camp. Kevin."*
Kevin and Darryl threw on their backpacks, which they had filled with food, water and simple hiking gear, and left the house. Leaving the compound quietly, they walked briskly down the road to town in search of a morning bus. Within minutes a pickup truck, the local private "bus," stopped, and the two climbed aboard. They paid the fare and rode into the heart of the city where they again caught another "bus" headed to the River Kwai Bridge and past the gold camp road.
Darryl knew the road they were looking for and signaled the driver. The pickup stopped and the

The Treasure of the River Kwai

boys jumped off, dragging their gear with them. As they entered the deeply rutted jungle road, Kevin pulled from his pocket the copy of the map key he had made. "I hope I got this right," he muttered as he examined the map. Kevin figured the map key showed a trail that started where the other map left off. *We'll probably never find the starting point exactly with all the digging that's been done,* he thought. *Whatever markings there were a year ago, or whenever, are long gone by now.*

"What are we looking for?" Darryl asked, interrupting Kevin's thoughts. Darryl was walking beside Kevin and trying to look at the paper in his hand. "Can I see that?"

"No. Never mind it." Kevin frowned. "It's just some notes I made . . . from a map of the area." Kevin had decided not to show the map to Darryl. He had studied it the night before, but the simple drawings and unfamiliar area made precision difficult. He stopped to take a look to get his bearings. *I hope I can figure this out,* he muttered to himself. "I guess we should just walk up this trail." The copy he made wasn't very good.

Poorly drawn from the original, the copy contained three individual drawings connected by lines, from a rough triangle around a center mark. The drawings seemed to be of three distinct geographical spots that had unique features. The first was a hill with tall trees, the second a river, and the third a rock wall or cliff near or beside the river.

"Let me look at it, Kevin," Darryl insisted again.

The Treasure of the River Kwai

"Just forget it, Darryl, will ya!" Kevin stuffed the paper back in his pocket. "It's nothing." The boys were perspiring heavily from the heat and humidity. Kevin wiped his brow and looked into the sky. He could see the sun burning through haze in the east. Fog hovered over the treetops in the distance. Monsoon rain clouds were forming to the south, probably coming up from the Gulf of Thailand. "We might get rain by noon, today, I think. . . ." Kevin adjusted the pack on his back and walked a little faster up the trail. "Are you ready to get wet?"

"No way!" Darryl shook his head vigorously and looked at the sky. "How do you know where we're going? Have you been here before?"

"Sure I have," Kevin said condescendingly. He turned to see Darryl staring at him. Kevin laughed. "No, Darryl. I've never been here before. I just looked over some maps before we came and made some notes. You've seen the treasure map . . . haven't you? Don't tell me you haven't seen it! It's been in newspapers all over Thailand."

"I don't read the newspaper much," Darryl confessed. "I only like the Sports section of the Bangkok Post, and that doesn't have much American stuff."

"Well, the map has been printed by everybody. Only problem is, everybody's been digging in the wrong place," Kevin explained.

The boys walked in silence, stepping carefully to avoid slimy brown mud in the ruts of the trail, and looking into the dense jungles on either side for clues, activity, anything. Then, after twenty minutes, they crested the hill and there it was. The gold camp

The Treasure of the River Kwai

spread out in a wide swath of scrub land, nestled in a small confluence of valleys and low rolling hills. What had once been plush jungle was now dirty, muddy ground, the size of two football fields. Only a few trees and bushes stood in the entire clearing and between most of these lines were strung for clothes and make-shift canvas tents. The standing tropical growth, thick and green, made a clear perimeter around the clearing. A few people, mostly men—as far as Kevin could see—were milling around engaged in various activities. Some stood over holes in the ground smoking and talking, others dug or poked around rocks and boulders. Some men were checking equipment scattered here and there over the area.

Kevin took a deep breath and sighed. "Well, I wonder where the **X** is," he muttered to himself.

Chapter 14
CAPTURED!

While Somsuk watched from the shadows at the edge of the jungle, the two boys emerged into the clearing and stood in the morning sunlight. To Somsuk, they seemed lost and unsure of themselves. *Hah! Foreigners!* He thought to himself with disgust. *They're afraid.* This would work to his advantage. He elbowed Kauwee and pointed, "There they are. See them?" Kauwee nodded and Somsuk continued, "We better move quickly before they start talking to everyone. Come on."

The two men stayed in the shadows and moved toward the Americans. Somsuk hurriedly sketched a plan. Kauwee would approach them from the front pretending he was a supervisor or local authority. He would engage them in conversation and put

The Treasure of the River Kwai

them on the defensive. If possible he should move them out of view, and then Somsuk would take them from the rear. They had no intention of killing them, at least not now. "But we can't let them get away," Somsuk emphasized. "We need them to find the gold."

Somsuk disappeared into the jungle brush. Kauwee moved out of the shadows and started walking toward the Americans as swiftly as he could on his fat legs. Kevin saw him coming and whispered to Darryl, "I wonder who that fat guy is. Maybe he's in charge of one of the camps . . . ."

"Yeah, maybe," Darryl answered. "Looks like he's coming this way. What are we gonna say to him?"

"Can you talk to him?" Kevin suddenly realized he was totally dependent on his younger accomplice. "You better find out who he is. Tell him we're just hiking around the River Kwai Bridge."

"What are you boys doing here?" Kauwee yelled in his toughest Thai voice. His voice squeaked despite his best attempt to hide his nervousness. "You're not supposed to be here."

"We're just out walking, sir." Darryl said in broken Thai.

Using his formidable size to compensate for his anxiety and the squeaky voice, Kauwee walked up real close to Darryl. "You must have a permit to be here. Do you have a permit?"

Darryl began shaking. "No. We didn't know we needed a permit." Darryl looked at Kevin in dismay.

Kevin poked Darryl on the side. "What is he saying?"

The Treasure of the River Kwai

"He says we need to have permission to be here." Darryl was trembling. "He asked if we had a permit. I said 'No.' Now what do we do?"

"Just relax, Darryl. Tell him we don't have a permit. Tell him we're just hiking around near the River Kwai Bridge, and we walked up this trail. We don't need a permit for that." Kevin looked defiantly at Kauwee.

Kauwee couldn't speak English but he understood Kevin's defiance. He walked over to Kevin and pressed up against him. "Listen you little cockroach foreigner. I could squash you between my two fingers if I wanted to . . ." Kauwee pushed his belly up against Kevin.

Kevin backed away. "Geez, what's your problem, man!" Disgusted and intimidated, Kevin didn't want to back down. "What did he say, Darryl?"

Wide-eyed in terror, Darryl looked at Kauwee and then back at Kevin. "He said, uh . . . he said. . . ."

"What's happening, Darryl!?" Before Kevin could finish, another man burst from the brush behind him. The man leapt onto Kevin and with one crack to the head, knocked him to the ground.

Darryl screamed. Kauwee whirled and slapped him hard on the face, knocking Darryl to his knees, where he held his face and began sobbing. Kevin lay semi-conscious near him. Darryl pulled himself to Kevin, shook him and whispered between sobs, "Kevin! Kevin! Are you OK?" Kevin groaned, but did not answer. Darryl looked up at the two men standing over them. The skinny man had a big scar on his face. In a confused mixture of English and broken Thai, Darryl asked them, "What do you want? We

The Treasure of the River Kwai

don't have a permit. Why did you hit him? We didn't do anything . . . Please, just let us leave. . . ."

Somsuk stood over Darryl and said, "Give us the map."

Darryl, repeating that they didn't have a permit, pleaded with the men to let them leave. He shook Kevin again. Kevin groaned and rolled his eyes.

"Shut up and look at me, you imp!" Somsuk ordered. He grabbed Darryl by the hair and shook him. "We want the map! We want the gold, and you are going to show us where it is! DO YOU UNDERSTAND ME, YOU STUPID AMERICAN?!"

Bewildered, Darryl looked through hazy eyes at the scar-faced man. "The gold? . . . What . . ."

"Listen, you stupid . . ." Somsuk cursed at the dazed and dirty adolescent. "We know about the gold and your special map. We've been following you and your friends for days. Don't play stupid with us. We could kill you just as easy as walk away right now. Where is it?"

Darryl couldn't understand everything the man said. Something about a map and following them, and . . . about . . . This couldn't be happening! We just came here to explore. Darryl looked up at the men, confused, disoriented . . . and then back to Kevin. He shook him again. *Kevin!* Why wouldn't Kevin wake up?

Kevin groaned and opened his eyes. He tried to sit up. "Oh, man. What happened?"

"WE WANT THE MAP!!" Somsuk hissed, his voice trembling with both anger and fear. Somsuk suddenly realized he was shouting. He looked around, afraid the ruckus with these foreigners

The Treasure of the River Kwai

might attract the attention of the miners in the area. No one seemed to notice the group of four crouched in the dirt at the edge of the clearing. Somsuk knelt down next to Darryl's face. Still grasping a tuft of Darryl's hair, he jerked the boys head, pointed at Kevin and said, "Tell *him* we want the *map*. NOW!"

Darryl, tears streaming down his face, and quivering from shock and fear, shook Kevin again, and cried, "Kevin! Wake up!

"What . . .?" Kevin rubbed his head. Dirt and leaves were crushed on his face and in his hair. He could hear voices near him and saw people around, but everything was confused and foggy. "My head hurts . . . What happened?"

"Kevin!" Darryl was still shaking him. "That man hit you. They say they want a map. They say they've been following us and want the map. What are they talking about? What's going on?"

Suddenly, hearing the word "map" Kevin came fully awake. "What!!?" He looked up to see two Thai men standing threateningly over them. Kevin sat up and rubbed his head. He pushed Darryl away. "I'm OK, Darryl. Tell them we don't have no map. We're just out hiking."

Kevin tried to get up. Darryl translated the message. Kevin knew they were in trouble, and decided to stall for time. He had no idea who these men were, but was sure they were in serious trouble. Kevin stood to his feet and looked the scar-faced skinny man directly in the eye. "We don't have a ma . . ."

Before he could finish the sentence Somsuk hit him directly in the face. Kevin's nose gushed blood, and he fell hard to the ground.

The Treasure of the River Kwai

"Oh my God, oh my God . . ." Darryl started screaming, and Kauwee slapped him, knocking Darryl to the ground beside Kevin. Kevin groaned, holding his nose. Blood, mixed with the dirt on his face, dripped down his mouth onto the front of his shirt. Somsuk wanted to hit the small one too, but Kauwee had already knocked him down.

Kauwee was shaking. "What are we going to do now? I don't like hitting these foreigners. They're just kids. We could get into big trouble. Someone is going to see us." He looked around the camp nervously. "We've got to get out of here before . . ."

"Shut up! We didn't come all this way to quit now. They have the map! I don't care if they are children. What did you expect? Did you think they were just going to walk up to us and hand us the gold!?"

Somsuk looked around at the camp. No one seemed to be paying any attention, but Kauwee was right. "Let's get them out of here," he ordered. Each grabbed one of the boys and pulled them to their feet. Kevin started to scream for help but Somsuk clasped his neck and punched him hard in the stomach. The blow silenced him immediately. He pulled a large shiny knife from his belt and held it up in front of Kevin's face. "Nee-ap!" *Quiet!* he hissed. Kevin, his eyes wide in silent terror, nodded. The men pushed the two boys into the jungles.

When they reached a safe distance from the camp, Somsuk gave the two frightened Americans the short version of his rules. He could kill them on the spot. He could let them live. It really didn't matter which way. What mattered was the gold.

The Treasure of the River Kwai

They wanted the gold, and these two were going to help them find it. They could give him the map now or take him to the gold. Either way, they weren't going to be released until the gold was found. If they tried to escape, they were dead, and Somsuk could make sure no one would ever find them.

Kevin listened gravely to the explanation as Darryl roughly translated each sentence. Darryl had regained enough composure to explain to the small man that he had to translate for his friend. *Please talk slow—I can't speak Thai well.* In an uncommon show of maturity he persuaded the man to speak slowly and give him time to translate for Kevin.

As he spoke, Kevin decided that their best alternative was to give the men the copy of the drawing he had and let them try to find the gold. He hoped that, in route, they would meet David and the gang, or someone else, or some opportunity would arise and he and Darryl could get away. He could see that the little man with the scar on his face was a real threat. The fat one would be easy to overcome if necessary. He couldn't yet determine what kind of friendship or relationship, if any, the two had.

"Here. Give this to them." Kevin pulled the drawing from his pocket and handed it to Darryl.

"What's this?" Darryl asked, taking the paper.

"Tell him it's a copy of a map I saw," Kevin said. "Tell him it's the only thing we have, and we don't know if it is accurate or not. We don't have the original. They can look in our stuff if they want, but we don't have anything else." Kevin hoped the paper would ignite enough interest in finding gold, that their captors would be distracted and therefore less hostile.

The Treasure of the River Kwai

"Tell them we haven't found any gold yet either. We don't know where it is. We were just out hiking."

The idea appeared to work, because when Darryl handed the paper to Somsuk and explained to him what it was, Somsuk's face immediately changed. He excitedly showed the paper to Kauwee and the two nearly danced for joy. Somsuk didn't respond to Darryl's explanation, but he knew the boys were telling the truth. They had had no time to find the gold before today. But now *he* had the map! Somsuk examined it hungrily. *I'm rich!*, he thought to himself.

After a few moments Somsuk returned to the task at hand, and ordered their hostages to lead the way towards the first checkpoint on the map. Somsuk figured he could decipher the map as easily as the Americans, except for the few words in English that were scrawled on the corner. He ordered Darryl to interpret these: *hilltop with trees, river,* and *cliff beside river.* The last entry—cliff beside river—Darryl could not translate, not knowing the Thai word for cliff. The best rendition he could muster was *big rock* and when the scar-faced man seemed satisfied, he let it go at that.

As the motley group made their way through the thick jungles, huge monsoon storm clouds gathered force in the distance. The only evidence of a change in the weather was the gradually fading sunlight. The sun, which had shined brightly in the camp that morning, was replaced by a steadily graying cloud cover that filtered through to the jungle floor. The air was also cooling and gusts of wind rustled branches overhead. The four hikers trudged slowly through the thick jungle brush, looking occasionally upward with apprehension at the approaching storm.

Chapter 15
SECRETS REVEALED

David jerked abruptly awake, hearing Kevin scream. He opened his eyes and realized he was lying on his back in bed. The ceiling fan slowly rotated above him. A child screamed in the yard again, and David remembered where he was.

Man, what a dream. What WAS that? David sat up. Wichai was still asleep in the bed beside him. Kevin was gone from the floor mat between them. David got up, pulled on a shirt and shorts, and walked down stairs. The kitchen clock read 6:45. The house girl had coffee ready. David took a cup— he wasn't in the habit of drinking coffee—but she handed it to him and so he took it.

"Cop koon," he said absent-mindedly. *Thank you.* The girl smiled meekly and resumed mopping

The Treasure of the River Kwai

the floor around the island cabinet in the center of the room. David leaned on the counter and took a sip of coffee. He saw the note and picked it up: *"Couldn't sleep. Darryl and I left early to get started. Will meet you at the camp. Kevin."*

"What!" David shouted, startling the girl. He ran up the stairs and called Wichai. Soon the rest of the Smith family gathered in the kitchen.

"I can't believe he did this!" David exclaimed, partly to himself and partly to the group. "I could tell yesterday he was upset that we were delayed in getting over to the river, but I didn't think he'd just up and leave with Darryl."

"Well, it's probably not that big a deal, David. The three of you should just get going and meet them," Sandy Smith tried to smooth down the youthful male competitiveness.

"It's more than that, Mrs. Smith." David hesitated a moment. He knew, with this development, he shouldn't conceal their plans any longer.

"What is it, David?" Kate asked.

"We found gold in Koh Samui."

Silence fell over the room. "Say that again," John Smith said.

"We found gold—a whole lot of it . . . in a treasure chest. . . ."

"What are you talking about?" Mr. Smith interrupted. His coffee cup, halfway to his mouth, hung suspended on his fingers in midair. The Smiths—John, Sandy, and Kate—stared at David, disbelieving.

"We were exploring a cave on an island in Anthong Marine Park, and, well, we found a whole

The Treasure of the River Kwai

bunch of gold—a big gold bar and lots of coins—in a treasure chest.

With everyone staring at David, John said, "OK, David. Tell us what happened—you know, the whole story."

"Like I said, we were exploring in Anthong Park and found a *treasure* chest in a cave! In the chest was a map, a special map that is like . . . well like a key, you know, that interprets another map. . . . The map key seems to be related to the gold hunt up here at the River Kwai." Stumbling at first, but then words began coming out more smoothly. "The map key, if it is what we think it is, is from a local legend. Wichai knows about it. His family is from this area. . . . We came here to follow the map and see if we could find the other gold. . . ." When David finished the story, John Smith whistled softly. . . .

"Wow . . ." Mr. Smith whistled. "Where's the gold now—the stuff you found?"

"We traded some in for cash to make this trip, and the rest we put in a safe deposit box in Bangkok. Wichai helped arrange it."

"Good. I'm glad you're not carrying it around with you." John walked over to Sandy, a worried look creasing his wife's face, and pulled her to his side. "David, what kind of guy is Kevin? Do we need to go look for him and Darryl?"

"Well, Kevin's OK. I think he'll be OK with Darryl." David tried to both defend his friend and also give some assurance to Darryl's parents that Kevin wasn't totally stupid. "I don't think he'd

The Treasure of the River Kwai

deliberately do anything dumb. He has been pretty caught up in the prospect of finding more gold, I guess. I kind of got caught up in it too. We didn't want to tell anyone. We figured the fewer people who knew the better."

"Well, you're probably right about that." John Smith agreed. "This could be real trouble if the wrong people found out. . . . How real is the map? Any idea if it's a hoax?"

"We won't know for sure until we follow it and see what we find." David said. "That's what we were going to do today. I guess Kevin couldn't wait to get on with it." David suddenly thought about the map in his pack. "I wonder . . . just a minute." David ran upstairs to his room and dug into his pack. He found the map in the backpack pocket where he put it. He ran back downstairs with it and showed it to the group. As John Smith studied the old, cracked piece of paper, David asked, "What do you think we should do, Mr. Smith?"

Sandy Smith spoke first, "The gold scares me, David. This is serious." She looked pleadingly at her husband. "You boys should not have gotten all wrapped up on this without telling your parents!"

"Well . . ." John Smith said, "I think . . . I guess . . . what we should do right now is drive you up to the River Kwai Bridge for the morning to go find Kevin and Darryl. When you find them, bring them back, no harm done. Then we'll talk about what to do next."

"Do you want to come with us?" David offered.

"Well . . . yes," Sandy said.

The Treasure of the River Kwai

"No," John interrupted. "I think you two should go and find them. I don't want to make this into a federal case . . . yet. When you guys get back, we'll talk. But let's get going right away, and then we can all meet again around noon at the bridge. Is that OK?" John looked at his wife and she nodded nervously.

"Sure, Mr. Smith. That's a good plan. . . ." David said. "And, I'm sorry."

"Look, David. If Kevin ends up finding a million dollars in gold with my Darryl, then maybe I'll . . ." Sandy finished the sentence with a wave of her hand. "Maybe nothing. You go get your stuff and I'll throw some food into a pack for you both."

"Dad. Mom. I'm going with them." Kate said firmly. "I had planned to go anyway, and I still want to go."

"Just let the boys do this, Kate," Sandy said, opening the refrigerator door. "You guys can be together more when they get back."

"It's just a hike along the river, Mom! Why do we have to make it any bigger a deal than that?" Kate prevailed after a few more words, with the stern warning from her Dad to stay with David and Wichai and *no running off on your own!*

After breakfast John Smith loaded the boys, Kate and their gear into the pickup truck and drove them to the River Kwai Bridge. Secretly he wished to join the group, and follow the map with them. Like it has done to men for centuries, gold fever—the ardor of riches—inflamed him. But in a conversation out of the other's hearing, Sandy persuaded him to let the boys go alone. *They should settle their issues*

The Treasure of the River Kwai

with Kevin first. Maybe later you can all go looking for gold together.

When they reached the road entrance that led into the gold digging area, John helped the youths with their backpacks. He told his daughter to behave herself and be nice to her brother when they found him. John Smith stood by his truck and waved as the three youths started up the dirt road into the jungle.

"So, where do you suggest we look for these guys?" David asked Kate and Wichai as they hiked up the road.

"There's only one place to look, David," Kate said. "We've got to follow the map. We go to the camp, find the starting point, and look for them along the way."

"We're not supposed to go looking for the gold, Kate. Your folks want us to find these guys and come right back. Anyway, Kevin's note said he'd meet us at the camp."

"Sure, but where do you think they'll be? They went looking for the gold." Kate was walking faster than David, and he quickened his pace to keep up with her. "They won't be at the camp waiting."

"They probably made a copy of the map," Wichai said, walking fast to stay beside David. His shorter stature made the going hard for him to keep up with the two, taller, Americans. "I don't think Kevin would do this without knowing where to go."

"OK. That makes sense. . . . Slow down a little, Kate. We need the energy to get through the morning," David adjusted his backpack and continued. "We'll go to the camp and then try to

The Treasure of the River Kwai

find the first landmark—the hill with the trees. We'll follow it 'till we find them."

****

While David, Wichai and Kate trekked toward the gold camp, only a short distance from them, out of sight and hearing, Kevin and Darryl, had found the first landmark. Their nefarious captors, with Somsuk leading the way and impatient to continue, pushed and dragged them through the jungles toward the River Kwai. Nearby, but out of sight because of the dense jungle in the lower areas, David, Wichai and Kate easily discovered the hill with the trees, by simply walking to the highest visible point in the area. From this position they could see, through the patchwork of clearings and jungle growth, the river below. Their descent to the river took them on a trajectory that passed Kevin and Darryl by only a hundred yards. Had either stopped to listen, they could have heard the crunching footsteps and voices of the other. But Somsuk and Kauwee, feverish for gold and pushing their captives in another direction, passed by undetected by David and his friends.

Kauwee was heaving air and perspiring heavily. He felt strained almost beyond endurance. He stopped and wiped his forehead with a dirty sleeve. *Water! Isn't there any water around here!?* Earlier he had forced Kevin and Darryl to surrender their backpacks. He consumed the food and water he found in them, and only shared the last third of the older kid's—*Keewin*—water bottle when Somsuk knocked it from his mouth. "You're drinking all the

The Treasure of the River Kwai

water, you idiot! Give that to me." Somsuk took the bottle and finished it. That seemed like hours ago, and Kauwee needed another drink.

"Get moving!!" Somsuk shouted at him. The skinny little man turned and stared up the hill at him. The two kids, just behind Somsuk, stopped and turned too. *What are you looking at, falang?!"* Kauwee thought. He wiped his face with a greasy hand and stumbled down the hill. The group continued this faltering descent towards the river, with Kauwee dragging behind.

Kevin looked behind him again at the fat Thai man. He thought of trying to escape, but was unsure he and Darryl together could outrun Scarface (the name Kevin had given the thin one out in front). Kevin kept walking as he considered the options. The fat man was no problem. But Scarface was more agile and he had that knife . . . *we could easily* . . . Kevin decided to wait for a better time. He tried to walk beside Darryl, pretending to give him assistance down the hill.

"We've got to find a way to escape," he whispered. "We can easily get away from the fat one, but I'm not sure about Scar-face."

"What do you want to do?" Darryl said, trying not to sob. His tears had stopped flowing and had dried into crusted, dirty stains on his cheeks. He tried to wipe them away, but only smudged his face more. "He's got a knife," Darryl said motioning to the skinny man ahead of them.

"Shut up, kid!" Somsuk whirled around and sprung at Darryl, fist raised. "You shut up! And tell that smart-mouth to stop talking too or I'll knock

The Treasure of the River Kwai

out his teeth! You understand me?!" Darryl nodded that he did.

"What did he say," Kevin asked.

"He said stop talking or he'll knock your teeth out."

Kevin nodded at Scar-face, trying to appease him with a sorry look. Somsuk resumed walking, but now stayed near, watching the boys. In this way the four made their way silently to the river.

Within minutes they heard the water flowing. Reaching a brush-covered embankment, they slid down to the riverbank. Somsuk immediately scanned the area, looking for the "big rock" on the map. Many large rocks marked the river. Somsuk began a haphazard search by climbing from rock to rock, stopping occasionally to inspect. Keeping frustrated eyes on the Americans behind him, and feverish for gold, he wanted to press ahead alone, but was afraid to leave the boys with Kauwee. *The idiot will let them escape!*

After a few minutes of fruitless searching, Somsuk returned to the group. Pulling out his knife, he pushed Darryl to Kauwee, whose face was puffy and dripping with sweat. He had abandoned his watch of the boys and had found a seat on a small rock on the riverbank.

"What is wrong with you!" Somsuk yelled at his partner. "I need some help." Somsuk pushed Darryl to the ground next to Kauwee. "Here. Hold this kid. Put the knife to his throat and if he even breathes heavy, kill him. DO YOU HEAR?!"

"Don't yell at me, Somsuk!" Kauwee shouted. "I can do it, but don't yell at me."

The Treasure of the River Kwai

This was the first time the two criminals had exchanged either one of their names in front of their prisoners. Somsuk glared at Kauwee. He wanted to kick him in the face and scream at him. *Now they know my name, you IDIOT!* He hoped the younger one hadn't noticed. "Did you hear what I just told him, kid?" Somsuk looked at Darryl who was sitting in wide-eyed terror beside Kauwee. Darryl nodded that he understood. "Tell your friend. Tell him not to run or you will die. Understand?" Darryl nodded. "Tell him now."

Darryl called to Kevin and explained the deal between sobs and shaking. Kauwee held Darryl with one arm wrapped around Darryl's neck. Kevin nodded to Somsuk and Kauwee.

In this way Kevin and Somsuk spent the next hour searching for gold in the wrong place while David, Wichai and Kate passed them by and found the cliff by the river where the gold was hidden.

Chapter 16

THE RIVER CAVE

The dark opening in the cliff face was hidden to David and his friends as they waded across the water. They were chest deep in the steady flowing river. *This has to be the final landmark*, David thought, looking at the cliff, standing in waist-deep water. They found this spot on the river by chance, for the map did not clearly mark the location of the cliff. The three crossed the river and stood looking at the cliff face, unaware that, only a few hundred feet downstream, Scar-face and the fat man were holding Kevin and Darryl at knife-point.

"They're not here." David said. Drenched after wading across the river, they stared at the cliff. The water, brown colored and warm, had given no relief from the jungle heat and humidity. The tropical air

The Treasure of the River Kwai

was still thick and warm against the approaching storm, and raised beads of sweat on David's face. He wiped his face on his wet shirt sleeve and looked at the clouds overhead. "The sky is getting dark," he said. "It's coming in fast." The wind gusted, briefly refreshing the trio. Thunder clapped nearby and the three could see the flash of lightning in the distance overhead. "I wonder where they are." David checked his watch: 9:05 a.m.

"We should check out the cliff," Kate suggested. She pointed at the wall about fifty feet in front of them, downstream and across the river. At that point the cliff rose directly out of the water. The river was wider there, and bended to the right. Kate waded into the water up to her waist and pointed at the cliff. "Look at that!" she said.

A hole in the rock wall, almost covered by the water, was faintly visible. Long vines and branches and large leaves of jungle growth, some of which grew right on the cliff face, hung down like a torn green mask. Large cracks covered the cliff wall. If the hole was indeed a cave, it was neatly disguised. "Do you see that hole, David? That might be a cave," Kate said, turning back to them.

"Yeah, I see it. Do you think that's it?" David said. Kate walked back out of the water. The three stared at the rock wall. Wichai was shaking. He had made it across the river only with the help and encouragement of his friends. The crossing, in what for him was almost neck-deep water, was terrifying. "I wonder if Kevin and Darryl went in there."

"How will we get in there?" Wichai asked. "The hole looks small. And the water is deep."

The Treasure of the River Kwai

"I can't believe Kevin and Darryl would go in alone." David said. "It would be an under-water entrance."

"Maybe that's why no one has ever found it." Wichai offered. "Who would ever look here?"

David pulled out the map key and stared at it. The drawing showed a rocky wall with a dark spot, like a cave mouth, on the wall. Squiggly shaped lines were scrawled across the opening. He had never really noticed them before—insignificant marks on an old drawing. Now, looking at the map and the actual site in front of them, it made sense.

"Look at this!" David said. He showed the map to Kate and Wichai. "These lines across the cave opening. I never really thought about them before. It's water across the mouth of the cave! The cave opening *is* in the water."

"Well, who's going in first?" Kate asked anxiously. "Let's get going." She swatted at mosquitoes that had started swarming around their heads. "Whatever we're going to do, we better do it fast. The mosquitoes are swarming. This heat is making them all go nuts." Kate dipped into the water and submerged up to her neck. The inlet was calm, but just to their right, in the flow of the river, the current pushed more rapidly past them. Kate glided through the pool of water to the rock face. She then pulled and kicked along the wall. When she reached the dark spot she stopped and yelled, "There IS a hole here! It's BIG! Look! The top of the hole just sticks out of the water! Can you see it?!"

David squinted. "How big is it? I can't see much from here."

The Treasure of the River Kwai

"Most of it is just under the surface. Probably over four feet around. I'm going to check it out."

David yelled, "Wait!" but Kate disappeared under the water. She was gone for a tense moment, then resurfaced and yelled, "It's a big opening! It goes way in. I didn't go in far, but we might be able to swim in."

"Just hold on, Kate!" David yelled.

"Maybe there's a room or something inside and we can come up for air!" Kate yelled back excitedly. She groped at the wall with her hands and tried to reach in the hole.

"Just wait, Kate! We need to look for Kevin and Darryl." David was torn. He brushed his blond hair out of his eyes, thinking. "Gosh, it's getting humid. The storm is coming."

No Kevin. No Darryl. *Where are Kevin and Darryl?* David wondered if Kevin and Darryl had reached this point and went into the hole already. Then they should go in too. David looked around quickly for any evidence that Kevin or Darryl had been here.

"Wichai, look around here for Kevin's or Darryl's backpacks. Maybe they hid them in the bushes or something. I'm going over to Kate."

"Are you coming?!" Kate yelled. "I'm going in again!"

"Wait, Kate! Wait for me to get over there!" David looked at the map key again. Nothing he could see on the map gave any more clues about what was inside the cave. When he looked up Kate took a deep breath and slip beneath the surface. "Hey, what are you doing?!" David yelled, but Kate's head disappeared

The Treasure of the River Kwai

beneath the surface. She kicked her feet through the surface and then disappeared. She was gone.

"I can't believe she did that!" David yelled. He turned to Wichai and handed him the map. "Here, hold this. I'm going over there." David pulled off his wet t-shirt and handed it to Wichai. "Maybe they went inside. Keep looking around. I'll be right back . . ." He slipped into the water and swam over to the wall where Kate had disappeared. Thirty seconds passed. David clung to the rock face and waited—it felt like an eternity . . . *Kate!*

"Can you see her?" Wichai yelled from the other side of the inlet.

"No! I can't see anything!" David searched the rock at the surface of the water. "God, where is she!" He reached down into the hole with one hand and tried to yell into the small opening above the surface. "Kate! Can you hear me!!?" The only response was the rippling of the water around the opening of the cave.

Suddenly, a large object bumped hard against David's legs and he slid backwards in the water. Kate burst to the surface. She gasped and yelled, "Ouch! What are you doing, standing right there? I couldn't see a thing!" Kate rubbed her nose and grimaced. "I smashed right into you!"

"Why did you do that, Kate!?" David yelled loudly at her.

"My nose hurts. Is it bleeding?" Kate rubbed her nose and looked at her hand.

"No. It looks fine." David frowned at Kate. "Kate, don't do that again! We're supposed to stay together! You hear? That was dangerous! You scared us half to death!"

The Treasure of the River Kwai

"I was fine. It's not that far in. I just went into the hole and followed the ceiling line until I felt it go above the water again. Probably ten or twelve feet in there. I figured if it went too far I could just turn around before my lungs started hurting." Kate shrugged at David. "Sorry . . . Anyway, the hole is real big."

"Look, Kate. We've got to stick together, OK?" David said. They both clung to the rocks and stared at each other. "I don't want any more misunderstandings or accidents. That wasn't smart." Losing Kevin and Darryl had dampened their "fun" adventure. "Let's talk about what we do first, OK?"

"Sure, OK."

"Let's go back over there and tell Wichai what's up." Wichai was standing by the water's edge, staring intently at the pair. The two swam over to him and waded out of the water.

"Did you find something?" he asked.

"Yeah! A big hole!" Kate said. She looked at David. "Now, can I tell you what else I found inside?"

"Let's hear it . . . Come on, what?"

"Well, there's a little room in there, mostly above the water," Kate continued. "I didn't climb out to look around. There's some light coming in from somewhere too. Not much, but it isn't completely dark either."

"Is there any way Kevin and Darryl might have gone in there?" David asked. "Is there a room or tunnel in there? Maybe they went in ahead of us?"

"No. I don't think so. I guess there might be something like that in there. But all I saw was a

The Treasure of the River Kwai

room. Like I said, I didn't get out to look around. It was kinda dark anyway."

"Well, wanna go back in and check it out?" David said.

"Let's go," Kate answered eagerly. She waded back into the water. She slapped a mosquito on her thigh. "Ouch! These things bite!"

"Davy, what shall I do?" Wichai stood tentatively behind, waiting. "I don't want to wait out here."

"Look, Wichai," Kate said soothingly. "It's not that hard to swim under water. It's sort of like taking a shower. You just close your eyes and hold your breath."

Wichai stared at Kate. "Taking a shower?"

"Well, yeah. We aren't even going to swim really. We'll just pull ourselves along the rocks under the water. . . . Here try this." Kate squatted down in the water, up to her neck. "Get down in the water like this." Wichai squatted down in front of Kate. "Now take a breath, hold it, and go under." Kate breathed in and slipped under the surface. She stuck her hand out of the water and gave Wichai the thumbs down sign, encouraging him to follow her, then popped through the surface. "See, easy."

Wichai looked at David in terror.

"Come on, Wichai." David said tersely. "This is the only way. You either do this, or you stay behind. I'm sorry. But if you want to go in, you've got to do this. Otherwise, you can stay here and keep your eye out for Kevin." David hated to push his friend, but there really was no other choice. Time was wasting.

Thunder rumbled in the distance, growing louder and closer. The monsoon storm moved steadily

The Treasure of the River Kwai

toward them. Wichai looked at the darkening sky and then back at his friends. He did not want to be left behind again. But the prospect of swimming underwater, and then into a cave, with the threat of a storm all around, required more daring than he could muster. "I'll stay here," he said reluctantly. "Just don't stay in there too long." He mumbled something in Thai and slowly waded to the sandy shore. David and Kate looked at each other. David shrugged.

"I'm sorry, Wichai," he said, "We won't be too long. It might be good, anyway, for someone to keep a lookout out here for Kevin and Darryl. We'll be right back."

Kate took the lead. They paddled to the cliff face and found the hole. The two clasped hands, not in a romantic gesture, although David's heart warmed touching Kate in this way. In unison they filled their lungs with fresh air and submerged. Assisting each other, they pushed and pulled themselves quickly into the hole, briskly grasping the rocks around them and scratching their feet along the bottom. Once in the hole, they separated and felt along the sides and top of the hole. Then the ceiling rose above them. Eager for air and claustrophobic in the dark, tight space, they burst into the cavern.

Gasping for air, David clung to the sides of the entrance and looked around in the small room. "Wow! This is amazing!" he exclaimed.

"Yeah, isn't it cool?" Kate pulled herself up onto the ledge in the room, letting her feet dangle in the water. The flat ledge, which was really the floor of the cavern, rose about a foot out of the water. "The light

The Treasure of the River Kwai

is coming in from up there," she said, pointing to a small crack about ten feet above them on back wall.

"Are there any other passages?" David asked. He pulled himself out of the water and sat beside Kate. "You OK?" he asked.

"I'm great!" Kate said. "This is amazing!" She stood and moved to the back of the chamber. The room was about 10-15 feet deep and about the same width. At the back Kate found another body of water. Ripples of current were visible in the dim cavern light. "No passages. But there is another pool of water over here! Look!"

David stood up. He had to bend over because the ceiling in the room at the edge of the water was low and jagged. He looked back at the water where they had entered. It looked like an underground channel. It flowed past where he and Kate had surfaced, narrowed and disappeared under rock. David walked over to the pool beside Kate. The pool was about five feet in diameter, almost a perfect circle, like a hot tub in the floor of the room. The young people looked around the room for a few moments, but, except for the faint light that trickled in from above, found nothing else of interest.

"Do you think something might be in there?" David asked apprehensively. He stooped down to inspect the pool. "The water seems OK."

"Maybe another passage to another room," Kate added. "Do you think that's possible?"

"Do you want to try?" David asked.

They stared at the watery hole, pondering their next move. David pulled a chemical light stick from his pocket. He removed the packaging, and bent

The Treasure of the River Kwai

it. The chemicals mixed and immediately the room filled with an eerie green glow.

"I'm going in there to look around." David sat down on the edge of the water and put his legs down into the pool. "The water is moving under there. Not strong, but it is moving. This must have some opening to the river outside, down in there somewhere. I wonder how deep it is."

"Be careful, Davy." Now Kate was nervous.

"Look who's talking! I just want to see what's down there." David lowered himself into the pool and went almost immediately up to his neck. "Man, I can't touch bottom in here. . . ." He felt around with his feet, hanging on to the top edge with his hands. "Hang on a minute." David continued searching around with his feet. He pushed himself under the water, using his hands for leverage. In a moment he resurfaced. "The bottom is right down there! About three feet over my head. See." David went under again keeping his hands extended above his head. His hands disappeared momentarily and then David came up.

"How's the current?" Kate asked. She bent down and reached into the water. "I can't feel anything moving."

"It's not bad really. There's a little movement at the bottom, but it's not rushing past or anything. I'm gonna try to swim down headfirst and see what I can find. Hang on." David disappeared under the surface. His feet thrashed out of the water and kicked the air, then disappeared. After a moment, David broke the surface smiling broadly. "Look what I found!"

Chapter 17
CONVERGENCE!

Kauwee needed a cigarette. He hadn't smoked in over an hour, and his head was aching. He fumbled through his clothes and pockets looking for the crushed, sweaty pack and cursed when he couldn't find them. *Must have lost them on the trail.* Kauwee wiped his brow. He looked angrily at the American boy sitting at his feet. Kauwee had given up trying to hold the boy by the neck. *Let Somsuk yell at me. I don't care.* It was too hot and both bodies were greasy with sweat and dirt. The boy was passive enough anyway. He sat quietly on the ground in front of Kauwee, mumbling to himself. *Maybe he's going crazy.* Kauwee didn't know what was wrong with the kid, mumbling on and on. Somsuk was out of earshot searching for the gold with the other

The Treasure of the River Kwai

American. *So what! Let him mumble.* He slapped his arm, killing a mosquito. Kauwee looked around wearily, but could see no sign of Somsuk and the other kid. He felt again into his pockets. *Where are those cigarettes!*

Darryl turned slightly to look at the fat man as he groped through his pockets. Darryl prayed, and sometimes the quiet appeals to God tumbled audibly out. He was trying to be quiet, mainly for fear of Scar-face. Scar-face was far across the river with Kevin, and the fat man seemed more concerned about cigarettes and food, so Darryl let his mournful prayers be heard. He was really scared. Darryl's prayers, mostly a repeated and panicked "Help me, Jesus," came out in an unintelligible stream. The fat man didn't seem to care. As he prayed Darryl squinted and looked across the river where Kevin had disappeared 15 minutes earlier. He wished for his glasses. Darryl couldn't remember losing them, but figured they must have fallen off when the fat man slapped him in the face at the gold camp. Since then everything was pretty much of a blur of green jungle. Even now it all felt like a slow-motion dream.

"Jesus, don't let them kill me or Kevin," he mumbled to himself. He looked cautiously at the fat man. The man's hands hung limply on his lap, his breathing was slow, steady. *He's sleeping! How did he fall asleep so fast?*

Darryl wished he could see better. He squinted at the blurry glare on the water, and wondered briefly if he should try to get away. But then he heard them. He couldn't see who it was, but from the sound was

The Treasure of the River Kwai

sure it was Kevin and Scar-face. They entered the water upstream and sloshed across. Darryl sat up and pressed himself deliberately against the fat man to warn him. It worked. Kauwee jolted awake. He looked down at the boy. Big drops of sweat dripped off his big nose. He muttered angrily and raised his hands to strike the kid but Darryl pointed to the water and avoided the assault. Darryl felt no sympathy for his fat, ugly captor, but he preferred to evade another one of Scar-face's tirades. To deliver the fat man from a verbal attack was to deliver himself. Kauwee looked down at the boy, wiped his face with his shirt sleeve, nodded and grunted.

"Are you sleeping?!" Somsuk yelled at Kauwee from halfway across the river. "I told you to keep you eye on him!"

"He is here and there is no problem. We are sitting here waiting! Don't yell at me! I'm tired of this." The fat man rested a heavy arm on Darryl's shoulder and stared at Scar-face, angry and defiant. "Did you find anything?"

"There's nothing over there. This must be the wrong place." Somsuk cursed and stared in disgust at the grimy boy. "This is the wrong place, kid. Tell him this is the wrong place." Somsuk gestured to Darryl to translate for Kevin.

After Darryl explained, Kevin said, "Ask him if I can look at the map again. . . . Are you OK, Darryl?"

"Yeah . . .I'm scared . . ." Darryl shuddered and his eyes brimmed. He wiped his face and blinked back tears. Darryl looked up at Scar-face and said, "Sir, he asks if we can see the map again?"

The Treasure of the River Kwai

Somsuk looked suspiciously at the two boys but pulled the crumpled piece of paper from his pocket. He handed it to Kevin. "You say this is not the original map. Where is the original map? Why is this one not the same?"

Darryl translated back and forth as Kevin explained to the man that the map they possessed was a rough drawing from the original. It was copied hurriedly and without much thought. They did not know how difficult it would be to find the gold. This was their first time in the jungles. How could they know?

Kevin stared at the map for a few moments and then, pointing at the third landmark, asked, "Darryl, what did you say this was?

"I said it was a big rock."

"Doesn't it look like a cliff to you?"

"No, not really."

"David's copy looked like a cliff, sort of. I didn't really make a good copy of it, but that's what it looked like to me. What did you tell the man it was?"

Darryl paused a moment and looked at Scar-face. The man was glaring at them. "I told him it was some big rocks."

"Tell him it looks like a cliff."

"I don't know the word for cliff."

"Well tell him that then, tell him it is big rocks, the side of a mountain, whatever. Tell him you don't know the words," Kevin could tell they had little time until Scar-face blew his temper again. Kevin wished he could smash the ugly faces of this sickly, scarred criminal and his fat accomplice. He would find a way, somehow, to get free of these . . .

The Treasure of the River Kwai

and Kevin cursed them in his heart. "Tell him now, Darryl."

Darryl slowly described the landmark, in his limited Thai vocabulary, and in a few moments Somsuk understood. "It's a cliff!"

Lightning struck hard nearby and thunder roared overhead. The four jumped and ducked down. "That was close," Kauwee exclaimed. "Let's get going, OK? Do you have any cigarettes, Som . . ."

"Shut up you idiot! Don't say my name again or I'll kill you, you stupid, fat slob." Somsuk glared at Kauwee. "Grab that kid and let's get going." Somsuk turned on the boys and spat at Darryl, "And you two—TELL HIM WHAT I SAY YOU LITTLE AMERICAN COCKROACH—IF YOU TRY ESCAPE I'LL CUT YOU BOTH BEFORE YOU TAKE TWO STEPS! DO YOU UNDERSTAND ME! I'LL CUT YOUR FILTHY THROATS!!" Darryl nodded at the red-faced man, and before he could translate, Kevin nodded too.

Anger, fuming anger, rose up in Kevin's chest, but he held his peace. He clenched his fists and heaved a slow, deliberate breath. *A better time will come. Right now they need us to find the gold.* Kevin took the lead, with Darryl one step behind him. Kauwee followed directly behind them. Somsuk followed at a close distance shouting directives, pressing the group downstream. The hike was difficult because the jungle grew thickly up to the riverbank. Large branches and vines dangled over each other along the river, competing for sunlight and space. Sometimes the four waded in the shallow water. At others, when the river deepened, they

The Treasure of the River Kwai

pressed through the green jungle wall and clawed and scraped slowly forward.

Downstream, unaware of the approaching group, Wichai waited. Nearly 15 minutes had passed since his friends disappeared into the cave. On the riverbank, all was quiet, except for the rumblings of the steadily approaching storm. Suddenly, as if from nowhere, the wind kicked up and rain, in thick, translucent sheets, came hammering down. Wichai jumped from his sitting position in grass by the river and rushed for cover. He cowered under the large-leafed undergrowth beneath the jungle canopy. In a futile attempt to stay dry he held his backpack over his head and pressed up against a tree. Within a minute Wichai heard voices, yelling at each other, and the sound of feet and hands crunching through the jungle behind him. He turned and saw four people, two Thai men and two foreigners—young white men—stumble out of the growth into the clearing not more than 20 feet away.

Wichai started to jump up to talk with them, but then stopped. He gasped. It was Kevin! In a moment he also recognized Darryl. Darryl looked haggard and frightened. *Who are those men? What are Kevin and Darryl doing with them?* Wichai waited and listened as the four stood in the downpour. They were soaked, water was dripping off of them—from their ears, nose, and elbows—but they stood like stony silhouettes in the pouring rain. One of the Thai men, the skinny one, looked around the area and shouted at Darryl. Wichai couldn't hear Darryl's reply. Darryl's voice was lost in the din of

The Treasure of the River Kwai

rain and wind. By contrast, the skinny Thai man's loud ranting came through loud and clear.

Kevin and Darryl are hostages! A million questions raced through Wichai's mind about how the scene in front of him could have happened. He wanted to jump from his hiding place and rush to his friends. But wisdom—and fear—held him by the tree out of view. Wichai strained to look across the pool of water towards the cliff. Heavy torrents blurred the cliff face. Wichai squinted and looked again. He hoped David and Kate would not at this moment emerge from the safety of the cave.

The Treasure of the River Kwai

Chapter 18
GOLD!

"Don't hold me in suspense!" Kate shouted. David floated neck deep in the pool of water. He cleared his eyes with his hand, and through the blur saw Kate leaning eagerly over the hole looking at him. She smiled. "Well?"

Faint yellow light rays from the cracks in the cave wall drifted across her hair and danced on his face and into his eyes. "What'dya find?!" she pressed again. David smiled broadly and raised his right hand out of the water presenting a glistening golden bar. Even in the dim light of the cave, the gold shimmered.

"Oh my gosh!" Kate reached and grabbed the heavy bar out of David's hand. The weight almost toppled her into the water.

The Treasure of the River Kwai

"Hang on to it, man!"

"Are there more of these down there?"

"Oh yeah . . . at least four or five more. I don't think there's a bunch. But there are more. Hang on, I'll be right back." David disappeared under the water and emerged a few seconds later with another bar. "Look at this!" He heaved it out of the water onto the side of the pool. Kate took the second bar with an *Oh my Gosh!* look on her face. She carefully laid it on the rock next to the first.

"David! We're . . . We're rich! We're rich! I can't believe this! Go get the others."

"Be right back." David disappeared under the water and returned with another bar, this time with report there were at least three more—a total of six bars. "I think there's a tunnel at the bottom that leads somewhere. I'll bet the real treasure haul is in there somewhere. Want to go check it out?"

Kate hesitated. The two stared at each other. "Do you?" Sobered by the reality of a pile of gold bars, more gold than she had ever seen, lying in front of them, and the possibility of more, momentarily stunned the two. "Look at this GOLD, David! It's so . . ." and Kate screamed with delight. "Let me in there to see."

"Be careful," David warned as he pulled himself out of the hole. "The tunnel is at the bottom, on that side of the hole, back there." He pointed to the far side of the small pool. "I left the chemical light down there under a rock so you can see."

"I'll be OK." Kate slipped into the hole and took a deep breath. She flipped upside down and disappeared with a kick of her feet. Moments

The Treasure of the River Kwai

passed. David sat quietly by the hole, staring at the glimmering gold. He shifted on the rock floor to get comfortable, thinking about events of the previous week . . . and his friends. *What happened to Kevin?* Even in the excitement of this discovery, David couldn't shake off concern for his friends. *I hope Kevin is all right. Why did he run off like that?*

In the brief silence, as he stared at the water waiting for Kate to return, David reflected. He had never really talked to Kevin about God. They went to school together. They sat through chapel and daily devotions with their "dorm family." Kevin knew where David stood on a lot of issues. But David had never openly explained the plan of salvation, or asked Kevin if he wanted to know more about Jesus Christ. *I guess I was looking for a perfect moment, or something. I hope he's OK.*

His daydreaming was interrupted when he noticed that the water near the entrance was rising and had begun to spill over into the cave floor. *The river's rising!*

Kate burst through the surface of the pool, gasping for air. She clung to the side of the pool while she caught her breath. Her face shimmered with astonishment. "David, it's phenomenal! There is a TON of gold in there!! Hundreds of bars, stacked up in a big room!!" Kate pulled herself out of the water, and continued the rapid-fire explanation. "The tunnel is real short. It goes down and then turns up and into a large, open room. There's light coming in there too. The ceiling is real high. I think the light is coming from the cliff face. I think part

The Treasure of the River Kwai

of that room is right above us." She pointed above their heads. "Up there."

David grinned and leaned back on his hands and whistled softly. "So . . . we found it . . . Wow . . ."

"I can't imagine how they carried all that gold in there." Kate continued. "They must have taken it in a little at a time, through this pool entrance. But there is a TON of it, David! Stacks and stacks. I couldn't count it. Maybe several hundred bars like these!!"

"I'm going in to take a look." David stuck his feet into the pool. "I'll be right back."

"Go ahead, but be careful. This scares me." Kate shivered and sat down on the rock floor.

"You, OK?"

"Yeah, I'm fine. I'm just cold. . . ." Kate said trembling. "There's no way to get all this out by ourselves." Kate looked at David. "It's too much, and it scares me. I want to get out of here. Fast. Hurry up."

"Do you mind if I go in and have a look first?"

Kate shook her head. "Just don't stay long. Look at me! I'm shaking—cold I guess, but I'm think I'm probably in shock too." Kate wrapped her arms around herself, pulling her legs up to her chest, and huddled next to the hole. "Go! And get back here."

"Be right back." David slipped into the water and dived. He found the tunnel. Just like Kate said. It went down and then curved upward. *It's like those plastic tunnels kids crawl through in playgrounds.* David's head pierced through the surface of the water and he looked around. The room *was* large,

The Treasure of the River Kwai

just like Kate described it! The ceiling rose high above him. Like the small room he had left, where Kate waited, light streamed in through small cracks above. The light danced on the floor. Gold bars glistened in three distinct stacks. There was nothing else in the room that David could see. *The Japanese must have discovered this cave. The perfect hiding place. It kept the gold safely hidden for 50 years! Why has no one ever come back for it?*

David pulled himself out of the water. He walked over to the gleaming piles and brushed his wet fingers over a gold bar. A layer of dust and dirt covered the bars, but still the heavy glow shined through. There was an inscription on each bar—some kind of numbering system he figured. David felt his heart pounding. He looked around, fearful, like a thief who had broken into a bank vault.

David and his friends had imagined finding treasure, and getting rich—youthful fantasies about mounds of gold and strings of pearls. Now, before him, in stark, gleaming reality, were mounds of gold laying stacked in neat piles. It boggled the mind. A chorus of deep glowing gold bars seemed to shout at him. David felt keenly out of place—and overwhelmed.

Feeling suddenly cold, David shuddered. He hugged himself and rubbed his arms. And then he realized something. In one of life's defining moments, when reality pushes dreams aside, David knew he and his friends would never extract these riches from the cave. The dream of gold was one thing. This was quite another. The task was beyond them. Physically, strategically . . . and morally.

The Treasure of the River Kwai

David laughed. *I wish I had a camera. Look at me!* "Hey Kate! Can you hear me!?" he shouted into the air. *A once in a lifetime moment. A TON of gold . . . and no camera. Man.*

The moment quickly turned to fear. This place wasn't safe! *What people might do to get this gold!* As he stared at the piles, a lifetime of wealth—to whomever could carry it safely out—he knew what he really wanted. He wanted to get back to Kate. He wanted to find Kevin. David looked down at the piles of yellow and hesitated. Feeling like a thief, he grabbed one bar—it was amazing how heavy it was—and jumped into the water. Taking a deep breath, he dove. In a moment he splashed through the surface of the pool. Kate was waiting for him, standing by the tunnel flow. She was staring at the water where they had entered the cave.

"Here," he said, handing the bar to Kate. "One more for the road."

"You were gone a long time, David. Did you find something else?" Kate asked. She looked worried.

"It's like you said, Kate. Tons of gold!" David said, pulling himself out of the water. "What's the matter?"

"The water, David. It's come up six inches in the last few minutes. I've been watching it. We gotta get out of here."

David walked to the entrance. "Oh, man. It *is* coming up!"

"I think it's raining outside. You can kind of hear it. Listen," Kate said. They stood quietly for a moment and could hear a slight whistling noise in

The Treasure of the River Kwai

the cave. "Hear that? "It almost sounds like wind." They looked around the room perplexed.

"Let's go, Kate. We gotta get outta here."

"I don't think we can carry more than one of these at a time," Kate said, lifting one of the bars. She tried to hold it in one hand. "Ugh! I don't know if I can hold on to this and swim too." She experimented with the bar, holding it in each hand, testing its weight.

"Just try . . .Let's go." David lowered himself into the exit channel. "Come on. The current is *much* faster than it was."

Kate eased her body into the water, struggling with a bar of gold. "Oh, man! Yeah, it sure is. It must be storming outside."

Trying to lighten the somber mood, David said, "Wichai is going to be mad. I'll bet he's soaked! But, maybe Kevin and Darryl have showed up . . ." Kate was still struggling with the gold bar. "Are you sure you can carry that? Maybe we should take just one this trip."

"No, I'll be fine. It's just hard to swim and hold it too. If it gets too tough, I'll just lay it down on the bottom of the channel and we can pick it up next trip."

"Fair enough. You go first and I'll help you if you need it," David said, offering his hand.

Kate moved around in front of David. She kissed him on the cheek. "For luck," she said. The two stared into each other's eyes, and for a moment fear dissolved into youthful love.

They took deep breaths and submerged, holding tightly to their treasure. The current was strong

The Treasure of the River Kwai

against them, much stronger than when they entered the cave. Swimming with one hand and kicking frantically, they struggled forward. At one point, Kate got stuck against the flow. David wedged his feet into the rock sides, dropped his gold bar, and pushed her forward. When she moved away, David groped frantically for his gold bar in the watery blackness. He found it, *finally*, and pushed forward, kicking harder. His lungs burned. *How much farther!?* David could no longer feel Kate's body near him in the dark channel. *She must be up there!* He kicked and grabbed the rock wall, desperately seeking handholds. The gold bar was *too heavy. Air! Air! Air!*

Kate burst through the surface first, gasping for air. Her arms splashed frantically, trying to keep her head above the water. Her lungs heaved in and out, and she drank in the cool, fresh air. David pierced the surface behind her, retching, coughing and grabbing at the water. He only used one arm, and clutched tightly to the gold bar with the other. When Kate saw him struggling she realized she had dropped her bar. *Oh, no!!* She kicked to the cliff face and grabbed onto the rough surface to rest a moment.

"Are you OK?" David coughed.

"I dropped my gold bar!" Kate sobbed. Hanging onto the rocks, she cried, coughing water out of her lungs and trying to hold back the tears.

"It's OK, Kate," David said. "It's OK . . . We got out." He looked at Kate. Clinging to the rock wall, she cried and tears flowed . . . *Oh, David!*

The water level was rising dangerously around them. It now completely covered the entrance. Rain

The Treasure of the River Kwai

poured hard against their faces. In the thundering downpour, David and Kate clung to the rocks and did not notice the four people standing along the edge of the water fifty feet away.

The Treasure of the River Kwai

Chapter 19
CONFRONTATION!

Standing on the riverbank in the downpour, Kevin turned toward the cliff and saw two people emerge from under the water. In the blur of rain and wind, he didn't immediately recognize them. They struggled on the surface, fighting against the current, trying to grab hold of the rock face. He almost yelled, "Look!" but then hesitated . . . They were . . . white faces!

It's David and Kate! My God! Kevin turned toward Darryl and the Thai men. He moved quickly around them to steer attention away from the cliff. It didn't work. Kauwee turned toward the cliff and saw them.

"What's that!" he shouted, pointing to the bobbing heads in the water. "Who are those people!?"

"Hold the boy!" Somsuk shouted to Kauwee, and ran over to the edge of the water. Kauwee grabbed Darryl and pulled him close. Kevin had the urge, in

The Treasure of the River Kwai

the brief moment Scar-face turned his back, to push the skinny man into the water and rush the fat one. But before he could make a move, the skinny one ran back to Darryl and pulled out his knife. "DO YOU KNOW WHO THAT IS?!" he shouted. Recognizing his sister, Darryl, now drenched in rain, shivering from the cold, and in near shock, nodded his head and quivered *yes*.

"WHO IS IT?!" Somsuk demanded. He moved closer and grabbed Kevin by the cuff of the neck.

"Tell him who it is, Darryl," Kevin said. Then, in a bold defiant move, he broke free from the scar-faced man's grip, and shouted, "IT'S OUR FRIENDS, YOU CREEP! WHAT ARE YOU GONNA DO NOW?! KILL ALL FOUR OF US?!" Kevin knew the man couldn't understand him, but he shouted anyway. "YOU CAN'T HOLD ALL FOUR OF US!"

Somsuk looked around frantically. He realized, with the arrival of two more people, his control of the situation was rapidly unraveling. He grabbed Darryl away from Kauwee, and wrapped his arm around Darryl's neck. Sticking his knife at Darryl's neck, he hissed into his ear, "Listen to me, kid. If you want to live, do as I say. And don't start crying! Do you understand?" Darryl nodded, his eyes wide with fright. "Tell your friend to STOP. NOW!"

Darryl shouted Kevin's name, and Kevin backed away slowly, eyes on Scar-face. "Good. Tell him to shout at those two in the water and tell them to come here."

Shaking uncontrollably, Darryl spoke so softly that in the pouring rain Kevin couldn't hear him. He had to walk up close.

The Treasure of the River Kwai

"What, Darryl?" Kevin said, keeping his distance. His eyes glared cautiously at Scar-face.

"Call them over. Please, Kevin," Darryl pleaded. "Do it. Please. Call them over." Darryl, his face white with shock, was shaking violently. "Please, Kevin."

"OK, Darryl . . . Don't worry. I'll do it. Don't worry. We'll be OK." Kevin ran over to the water's edge and waved his arms. "David! Kate! We're over here. Come over here! Quick! Please!" Kevin waved his hands wildly and yelled at the two in the water.

David and Kate, hearing Kevin's first outburst a few moments earlier, and knowing something was wrong, had lingered near the cliff face.

"What's going on?" Kate said, looking apprehensively at the four people on the river bank. "Who are those Thai men?"

"Something's wrong," David said. "Stay here, Kate, and let me go over and check it out."

"No, I'm coming over."

"Kate, please. Stay here. Just stay right here. We don't know what's going on, but until I find out, stay here. Please . . ." David's pleading look convinced Kate, and she nodded.

"Here, hold on to this." David handed his gold bar to Kate. "Maybe we can use it if there's trouble. Keep it under the water out of sight. And stay here!"

Kate clung to the rock wall, while David swam across the lagoon and sloshed out of the water. Scar-face stood by the water's edge, holding tightly to Darryl.

"Tell him to make the girl come over here," Somsuk whispered to Darryl.

The Treasure of the River Kwai

"Let him go," David said. "I speak Thai."

Somsuk looked at David with shock. A sickly snarl came over his face. "Tell the girl to come over here."

"Why should I do that?" David asked, trying to keep his calm.

"Because if you don't, I'll cut this kid." Scarface pulled Darryl closer and drew the knife up to Darryl's neck. "Tell her to come over here."

"What do you want?" David asked, stalling. "Are you looking for the gold?"

Somsuk's eyes brightened. "Yeah, that's what we're looking for. Did you find it?"

"Yes, we found it. If you let him go, I'll tell you about it. He's just a kid. I'll give you the gold we found, and you can go in and get the rest yourself. Just let him go."

Kevin walked over beside David. "They caught us at the gold camp, David. I'm so sorry. Tell him to let him go."

"I just did . . . Are guys OK?"

"STOP TALKING AND DO WHAT I SAY!!" Somsuk wrenched Darryl around and appeared about to stab him when David answered . . .

"OK. Don't hurt him. We already have one gold bar. We'll give it to you. I'll call her over here. Just don't hurt him." David turned and waved frantically his arms. "Kate! Come here! Come on! Bring the gold! NOW!"

Kate let go of the rocks and began moving across the water. She had difficulty swimming because of the weight of the gold bar. He looked at the Thai man and said, "I need to go help her. She's carrying

The Treasure of the River Kwai

a heavy gold bar. I won't try to escape. The boy is her brother. OK?"

The man nodded. Motioning at Kevin, Somsuk said, "Tell your friend to back off and sit down over there." He pointed to the rocks nearby. He called Kauwee, "Come over here and help me!" Kauwee cautiously moved over next to Somsuk. "Hold this knife on the kid," Somsuk ordered. "If anyone tries anything, stick him!"

The main thing now, David thought, *is to get Darryl away from that man. We outnumber them . . . Who are these men?* David looked carefully at Darryl, and moved into the water and swam toward Kate. She was progressing slowly towards them.

"How're you doing?" he said when he reached her.

"I'm exhausted. Take this," Kate handed the weight to David. "What's happening?"

As they swam to shore, David explained the little he knew. "I don't know who they are, Kate, but they look desperate. They're threatening to hurt Darryl, they want this gold, so we've got to get back there quick."

"Is Darryl all right?" Kate asked, worried. She looked toward shore and they swam faster.

"He's in shock, but I don't think they've hurt him. Kate, listen to me. When we get there, just stay quiet. And only speak in English. Don't let them know you speak Thai."

Somsuk stood by the bank of the river as David and Kate struggled out of the water carrying their treasure. Somsuk's angry grimace turned briefly into a hideous grin when he saw the gold.

The Treasure of the River Kwai

"Give me that!" He yelled, and grabbed the gold out of David's hands. He raised it up for Kauwee to see. "Look! The River Kwai gold! We found it! We're rich!" He laughed and began babbling in Thai, laughing and cursing. Rain drops and spittle dripped from his face and dropped to the muddy ground. "We're rich!" After a moment, he turned back to David and said, "How much more is in there?"

"There's more. Why don't you go in and get it? You don't need us anymore. Let the boy go. You can have the gold."

"Go back and get the others for me." Somsuk put one threatening arm around Darryl.

David hesitated for just a moment. He looked at the scar-faced man standing in front of him. *What happened to this man that he became such a monster?* David knew this man could hurt Darryl, but he also knew the two were outnumbered. Stalling, David looked around. Kevin was sitting on the rock nearby, seething with hostility, poised to jump on the man. Darryl, in shock, stood limply in front of the scar-faced man. Kate waited quietly behind David, shivering from fear and the swim. *She's safe, for the moment.*

"The water is coming up fast. I can't get back in there alone. I can't go and get all the gold out before the river rises too much."

"Go in and try."

"Look, sir. You are obviously an intelligent man. You can see what is happening here. The river is flooding. If we all go," David pointed to Kevin, himself and the scar-faced man, "we can get a few more out

The Treasure of the River Kwai

for sure. Your friend can hold the boy until we come back."

"No! You and the other boy will go!" Somsuk pointed to Kevin. "The girl will stay here with me." Somsuk signaled to Kauwee. "Come over here and hold her."

"NO!" David shouted. "You stay away from her!" and he backed up next to Kate. *Where is Wichai?!* He thought.

"I'll cut the boy!" Somsuk shouted. "Back away from her!"

"No! We will help you, but you must go with us." David stood his ground beside Kate. Somsuk hesitated. He knew time was running out. The river *was* rising. He could see it. Rain was pouring down. This monsoon could drop rain for 24 hours. All chance of getting any more gold today would be lost. If one of this group escaped, the gold would be lost to him forever. Somsuk knew he could not hold these kids much longer. Someone would escape. He also knew he couldn't kill anyone—he wasn't a murderer—and even if he knifed the kid, the others would get away. They might even attack him. His only hope was to retrieve enough gold to escape and run—run somewhere far away—far from Kanchanaburi, far from Kauwee, far from the mafia bosses to whom he was in debt. *Perhaps I should just run with all the gold. I can buy my escape. But I need more gold . . .*

"Kauwee!" he shouted, "Come here and hold the boy! We are going across the river to get more gold. Hold him!" Then to David he said, "Tell the girl to sit down here. Tell her no talking—NONE! Do you understand?!" David nodded. "The three of us

The Treasure of the River Kwai

will go and return. IF I DON'T COME BACK IN 15 MINUTES, KILL THE BOY!" he shouted to the whole group.

    Kate sat down cross-legged on a rock near where the man had pointed. David, Kevin and the Thai man waded into the water and swam across to the cliff. Remembering Wichai, Kate looked around for him. She hoped he was hiding nearby. Maybe he would help them. She shivered, pulled her knees up to her body to keep warm. She turned to check on Darryl. The fat man was staring at her. Kate stared defiantly back at him until he looked away. When she turned to look at the cliff, the three had reached the rocks and were hanging on, preparing to submerge. Kate couldn't see the opening. One head disappeared, then another, and then—it looked like Kevin—the final head submerged and was gone.

    At that moment Wichai whispered from the trees. "Kate!" he hissed. "Kate. It's me, Wichai. Don't turn around. Don't move! If you can hear me, shake your head." Kate nodded. "I'm going to go around behind them. Stay here. Come help me when you see me. OK?" Kate nodded again. Fear and exhilaration pulsed through her body. "Listen to me, Kate," Wichai continued, whispering, almost hissing through the downpour. "There is a big stick behind you. When you jump up, grab it. OK?" Kate nodded again.

    Oh, God! I can't do that! What is Wichai talking about?!! Kate shifted to look for the stick. *What stick? Am I supposed to hit that fat guy with a stick?!* Before she had time to think about it any further she heard a crunch.

Chapter 20
ESCAPE!

Kate heard a dull thud and whirled around just in time to see the fat man crash to the ground on top of Darryl. Darryl fell hard into the mud and the fat man, an unconscious mass, sprawled heavily on top of him. Wichai grabbed Darryl's hand and dragged him out from under the immense legs and arms. The fat man lay motionless in a puddle of muddy water.

"Darryl!" Kate ran to her brother and hugged him, holding him close. Darryl's arms hung limply by his side. "Are you OK?"

"Kate . . . I'm cold," Darryl said meekly. Then he suddenly snapped out of the lethargy and said, "You better get that knife away from him."

Wichai fished around in the water and checked the fat man's hands. He found the knife about five

The Treasure of the River Kwai

feet away. "I must have hit him hard! I hope he's OK." The fat man moaned. Wichai checked his head and found no blood. "I guess he'll have a headache for a while." He laughed nervously.

"Look what you did," Darryl said to Wichai, who was dwarfed by the large human laying big and round next to him on the muddy river bank. "It's like David and Goliath."

"From the Bible, yes?" Wichai asked.

"What do we do now?" Kate asked.

"We've got to get out of this open area and hide," Wichai said. "That way, when they come out of the cave, they won't know what happened. And maybe David and Kevin can get away."

"Good idea." Kate took Darryl's hand and led him into a hiding place in the jungle growth. They found a protected spot that allowed a view of the cliff. She helped Darryl settle there, assured him that she would be back, and returned to the riverbank. Wichai guarded the fat man, who was regaining consciousness. Kauwee pushed himself up from the mud and looked around. His hair hung disheveled over his face. His lip was bleeding and he could feel a painful lump growing on the top of his head. He rubbed it as Wichai stood over him with a stick.

"You have two choices, sir. I hit you again, or you can take that gold bar and leave right now." The fat man looked at the new Thai face standing over him—*Where did you come from?* He rubbed his eyes and looked again in bewilderment. Mud was caked to his fat cheeks and dripped off his chin.

The Treasure of the River Kwai

"Did you hear what I said?" Wichai repeated. Then, bluffing, he added, "The police are on their way here. Take that gold and get out of here! This is your only chance."

Earlier, watching the fat man from his hiding place in the bushes, Wichai had concluded he would be easy to overcome. The man was tired, hungry, and basically stupid. Getting him to forsake their ruined plan, especially with an offer of gold, would guarantee his departure. *He'll want to save himself—he wants some money too. Definitely the easiest plan.*

It worked. Kauwee stumbled to his feet and swayed dizzily. He looked incredulously at the American girl and the young Thai man standing before him. *Who are these people?*

"Get out of here!" Wichai shouted again. The fat man rubbed his aching head. He grabbed the gold bar from the ground, and without a word, waded across the river into the jungles. "Don't come back!" Wichai called after him.

The three youths settled into their hiding place. There, keeping a watchful eye on the cliff face, they waited quietly for David, Kevin and Scar-face.

"Wichai?" Kate asked, "Do you know who those men are?"

"I don't know," Wichai said, puzzled. "I've been thinking about it, but I don't know. Maybe somebody in Bangkok told them about us and they followed Kevin and Darryl. Maybe Kevin and Darryl talked to them in Kanchanaburi and they followed them. I don't know."

"There they are!" Kate exclaimed, pointing to the cliff. One. Two. Three heads popped to the

The Treasure of the River Kwai

surface. They struggled and thrashed in the water. Kate couldn't hear them from this distance with the pounding of the rain, but she saw them gasping for air. Kate winced. Her chest tightened and her hands clasped around a rock on the ground. *Come on, David!* The three men grabbed onto the cliff face and rested a moment. One of the three—it was David!—looked toward the river bank. Kate could see his face staring straight toward them. Then another looked. Soon all three were staring at the riverbank.

From the rock wall, Somsuk peered through the rain and stared in shock at the empty bank. *Where are they?* He wiped his face with his free hand and kicked hard to counter the downward pull of the gold bar he held in his other hand. The current pressed hard against his back. He quickly grabbed the wall again to stay afloat. Somsuk cursed, and screamed into the air. *What happened to Kauwee and the kid? Where's the girl!! Where's Kauwee!* Trembling with rage, he cursed his partner, the Americans who had tricked him, and, above all, his bad luck. They were at the doorway of riches, and Kauwee disappears! *The fool! If he could have seen the gold. Gold! Unbelievable stacks of gold! Ours for the taking!* Somsuk gripped the bar in his hand. *Where are they?*

Fatigued and angry, Somsuk pushed away from the rock wall and struggled toward the empty river bank. "You! Come with me!!" he shouted behind him to Kevin and David. They too saw the deserted bank. They too were shocked—and frightened—by the sight, the absence of Darryl and Kate. But the

The Treasure of the River Kwai

new development, although upsetting, was instantly liberating. They now followed the scar-faced man, not to obey his orders, but to investigate what had happened to Darryl and Kate.

Somsuk waded out of the water, clinging to the gold bar with both hands. At the edge of the water he bent over, heaving for air. "Kauwee!" he shouted as he trudged forward, "Kauwee! Where are you?!" He turned back to David and Kevin who were still in the water, swimming slowly across. "You! Get over here!" He looked around again. "Where did they go!?" he demanded.

David and Kevin stopped swimming, and let their feet find the bottom. There they stood, fifteen feet from the bank, chest deep in the water, holding their gold bars under the water. "We don't know where they are," David said. "How could we know?"

"Bring that gold to me!" Somsuk yelled.

"NO!" David yelled back. "Why should we obey you anymore?!"

"GIVE ME THAT GOLD!" Somsuk screamed. He turned around. "Kauwee!! Kauwee!!" He shouted into the air, no longer caring that he called his partner's name. "WHERE ARE YOU, YOU FOOL!!?"

David and Kevin looked at each other and strode boldly out of the water, keeping some distance from the skinny man. They clung to their gold bars, holding them close.

"Give me that gold!" Somsuk demanded again.

"Come and take it from us, you wretch!" Kevin shouted. "Tell him what I said, David. . . . COME TAKE IT FROM US, YOU UGLY CREEP!"

The Treasure of the River Kwai

Standing in the pouring rain and looking at the pitiable man in front of him, who only moments before he had threatened Darryl's life, David shook his head. "No!" he shouted back. The man's partner was gone, his weapon lost, and the man with the ugly scar on his face was alone. He stood in the monsoon deluge pathetically clinging to a bar of gold. David no longer feared this skinny little man with the rough voice and ugly scar. He felt contempt for him for what he had done to his friends—but now that they were free of him . . . at least he hoped so . . . *God, I hope Darryl is safe—and Kate! Where is she?* David looked at the man with a mixture of anger and pity.

Bracing himself, David said, "Sir, we are servants of God, who sent us to your country to bring good news to your people. My friends and I came here looking for gold today. That is true. But the gold belongs to your nation. We don't claim all of it for ourselves, and it's not all yours either. We have done nothing wrong, but you have threatened us. You have threatened a young boy. God sees what you have done, yet He cares about you."

The man stared incredulously at the foreigners, his eyes moving back and forth from David to Kevin. His eyes turned to the deserted riverbank, the flooding river, the jungle . . . "Kauwee! Where are you!!?" he screamed. He took a step into the water toward David and Kevin, "You . . ."

"NO!" David said, trembling. The gold was heavy in his hands. "We will not help you anymore! Don't try to take this gold from us. You cannot overcome two of us. Your friend is gone. Our

The Treasure of the River Kwai

friends are gone too! Leave now! Take the gold and leave!"

Somsuk stood ankle deep in the water, rain dripping off his face. He looked at the two young foreigners who dared to stand up to him. *God is watching?! What God is he talking about? The Christian God? I'm a Buddhist! And the Buddha never cared for me, nor answered my prayers. My life is nothing, and if I die today, who would care? Does God—or anyone—care?* Somsuk looked at the gold bar in his hand. It was more money than he had ever seen in his life. It might buy his freedom from the mafia. Was it enough? The other gold bar . . . the one he laid on the ground near Kauwee . . . it was gone. *Kauwee probably took it! I guess he's smart enough to know when it's time to run.*

Somsuk grinned sickly at the boys standing in the rain, up to their chests in the flooding river. *It's hopeless. Today at least. Maybe I can come back and get more of this gold—if no one finds out. Goodbye you stupid Americans.*

Without another word, Somsuk turned and walked upstream along the riverbank and stumbled across. The boys stood in the water quietly watching him go.

"What happened to Kate and Darryl?" Kevin said first. "Where are they?"

"We're here!" a voice shouted from the bushes. Kate burst out of the jungle and lunged toward David and Kevin. "Are you guys OK?"

David and Kevin sloshed out of the water and dropped their gold bars on the bank. "We're fine,"

The Treasure of the River Kwai

David said. Where's Darryl? And . . . what about Wichai?"

"In here, Davie!" Wichai yelled from the bushes. "Darryl's in here too."

"Darryl's moving a little slow right now, Davie" Kate said. "I think he'll be all right, but he's pretty shook up."

Wichai and Darryl emerged from the jungles and joined their friends on the riverbank. "You OK sport?" Kevin asked.

"Sort of," Darryl said. "I'm cold. Let's go home . . . I'm hungry."

"It can't be too serious if he's hungry," Kate tried to laugh.

"What happened?" Kevin asked.

Kate explained how Wichai overcame the fat man—*his name is Kauwee* David interrupted—and freed Darryl. When she finished, the five young people stood, fatigued and filthy, in a loosely defined circle near the river bank. Torrential rain pummeled them from above and gusts of wind struck at them from all sides.

"I'm really sorry . . ." Kevin said, breaking the silence. "I'm really sorry, David . . . I got impatient . . ."

"It's OK, Kevin," David replied. "I'm just glad you both are all right."

"It was a stupid and selfish thing to do."

"Let's go home," David said.

"Wait!" Kate said. "Can we swim back over there and get my gold bar?"

"No thanks!" Kevin said. "I'm tired of drowning."

The Treasure of the River Kwai

"Then, I'll go," Kate said, "I want to get one more."

"The water is deep, Kate. And the current is picking up," David cautioned.

"Then help me!" Kate said, and she walked into the water and started swimming.

"What to do!" David looked at Kevin and Wichai. They both shrugged.

The Treasure of the River Kwai

Chapter 21
SAFELY HOME

"The man at the embassy says the total haul is worth over three and a half million dollars." John Smith said. He sat at the table with his wife Sandy, and their children. David, Kevin and Wichai sat across from them. "And they're not sure this is the only stash location. There might be more in those rocks."

"We still can't believe you guys did this . . ." Sandy interrupted.

John nudged her. "And the total value of the stuff you guys found . . ."

"Including the third bar you insisted on going back for, dear," Sandy pinched Kate, who shouted, "Hey!" and jumped backward.

"Are you guys finished?" John frowned teasingly. ". . . *after* the Thai government takes their required

The Treasure of the River Kwai

portion, is worth about 80,000 dollars. Divided evenly—as you all agreed—between David, Kevin, Wichai and one share for our kids, each share is worth $20,000."

"Yee-ha!" Kevin shouted. "Man, I can buy me a new SUV when we move back to the States! When do we get the money?"

Everyone started talking at once until Mr. Smith interrupted, "OK, OK everybody. For your information, except for you Wichai . . . Wichai, you can do as you please with your share . . . All the American mothers and fathers have agreed that the money goes into your own personal college fund. . . ."

A chorus of groans ensued and Mr. Smith continued, "It will be sent to the parents, probably in a month or so. The Thai government gets the bullion for historic and archeological evaluation first. We get fair market value for the portion you found and carried out." More groans and boos . . .

"Wait, wait, wait!" John Smith held up his hands and continued, "With one exception . . . The parents have agreed to allow each of you to keep $1000 for spending as you wish." A hale of yelps and hoorahs followed.

"What happened to the two Thai men?" David asked. The room immediately returned to somber quietness.

"Well, the fat one you called Kauwee probably gave up the news of the gold. Apparently he took his gold bar to a dealer in Kanchanaburi for appraisal, and within a day the news was public. He disappeared soon afterwards. Makes

The Treasure of the River Kwai

me wonder if he wasn't killed by the mafia over his debts."

"As soon as the news was out, the gold camp and all the speculators and their workers moved—lock, stock, and barrel—to the new location. After the rains quit and the flooding went down, they got in and opened up the cave with dynamite. Hauled it out on boats. There was a lot of fighting, some violence, among the groups over claims. The government finally stepped in with a special police unit and took over. There's been order there ever since . . . and probably some corruption."

"What about the other Thai man, the skinny one with the scar?" David asked.

"Yeah, Scarface," Kevin said.

"They found him, dead, in the cave," John said. The room went silent.

"What!?" Kevin exclaimed. "How . . . what do you mean?"

"When they sent the first group in—they went in like you did. Swam under water through the tunnel. They found him drowned, under water, in the tunnel. It looked like he'd been in there for several days."

"He must have gone back," David said. "He waited for us to leave and he went back."

"That's what it looks like. The allure of all that gold was too much. He couldn't let it go, and it killed him." John Smith folded his hands. "I'm really glad you are all safe."

The room was strangely hushed while the young people relived the events of that day at the cliff face. Each one reflected on his experiences.

The Treasure of the River Kwai

Each had felt the intoxicating ardor of gold, and instant riches. Scarface *could* have been one of them. They had assumed he was different, but now, after this, the differences seemed less significant. They were more like him than they wanted to be.

"So, who gets all the money?" Kevin asked, breaking the silence. "I feel real sorta guilty about wanting more of it."

Everyone laughed. David and Darryl punched at Kevin from both sides. "OK, OK, I give up. I don't want anymore gold!"

"It'll all be settled in court, I'm sure." John suggested. "The people who worked to get it out will lay some claim on it. Other South East Asian governments—remember some of the gold came from Burma and Malaysia—will probably make a claim too. It's anyone's guess whether Thailand will honor that. And then, of course the Thai government will have their own agenda, because some of the gold is Thai . . . they'll probably find some way to keep most of it."

"Well, I'm going to enjoy my thousand bucks!" Kevin said. "I earned it."

"Yeah," Darryl echoed. "Hey Dad, do Kate and I like get $1000 each, or do we have to split it?"

"We split it, Darryl. 50-50 . . . It's better than nothing." Kate muffed up Darryl's hair. He ducked and pushed her hand away with a *Knock it off!*

As the group mused over how to spend their play money, Kate motioned to David and they walked out onto the front porch and sat down together on the steps.

The Treasure of the River Kwai

"You, OK?" Kate asked after they had sat a moment. They both stared out into the front yard where a few orphan children were playing under the watchful eye of a Thai worker.

"Yeah, I'm fine . . . Quite a summer, huh?"

"No kidding . . . You sure know how to show a girl a good time." Kate said, and they both laughed.

"It's good to see Darryl's doing OK, Kate . . . How's he been this past month?"

"He went to several counseling sessions in Bangkok, and my folks say they'll probably have him see a counselor in America when we leave next week. I think he'll be fine. He had nightmares for the first week, pretty bad. But that seems to be over now."

Kate propped her chin on her hands and balanced her elbows on her knees. "I have mixed feelings about going to America."

"Why?" David looked at Kate. "I thought you were looking forward to it."

"I was. But now, with all this stuff, and Darryl, we plan to stay longer. Maybe a whole year. I mean, Darryl seems to be doing fine, but they want to be sure . . . I'll do my junior year in a school in the States. Then I hope we come back so I graduate from Dalat. I really want to graduate with my class here—at least most of the kids. You're going back to graduate this year, aren't you?"

"Oh, yeah. I'll be there all year. I'm sorry you won't be there. That's a bum, Kate. I'll miss you."

"Really? I'll miss you too, David. . . ." They looked at each other and smiled. Kate took David's hand. "I'm glad you guys came back up to see us.

The Treasure of the River Kwai

Dad hoped you could. It's more fun this way than having to talk about everything over the phone."

"Yeah, we wanted to come. Kevin's folks paid for him to fly up from Surat. I hadn't seen him since the day we left Kanchanaburi . . ." David paused reflectively. ". . . after everything happened. The day we got back to my house he called his folks and they came up to Bangkok to meet him. Everyone was pretty shook up."

"What's Kevin going to do now?" Kate asked. "Sounds like he might not come back to Dalat this fall either."

"Well, his Dad got offered a job with USAID in Sri Lanka," David said. "Same kind of work—developing shrimp and fish farms—so they're looking at it. Kevin says they will probably go back to the U.S. for a few months for orientation, and then move there after the first of the year. They're leaving in a couple of weeks. He might still attend Dalat as a boarding student."

"How's he doing?"

David thought a moment. "This whole experience shook him up. We talked on the phone and at one point he said the he was really thinking about God a lot more now. Before this he just thought the whole religion thing was weird, but now he says he wants to talk with me some more about Jesus, and what it means to be a Christian. I hope I can say the right thing."

"That's great, David . . ."

"Yeah, pray for him . . . Kevin's a good friend."

"Did you know that Wichai's family is making some claim to gold too, Kate?

The Treasure of the River Kwai

Kate shook her head, so David continued. "You know, it was mostly because of him that we knew about the map key. And he was the first Thai—not including the criminals—who found the gold. I don't know what might happen, but, like your Dad said, the government has said that everyone involved, not just the people who dug it out, will get a portion. It makes me wonder if we might get some more too. I really doubt it, simply because we're foreigners. But, who knows. I think Wichai should get something more, because of his family's involvement."

Well, what are you gonna do with your money?" Kate looked at David and punched him. "Any more adventures?"

"Maybe. I told Kevin if he goes to Sri Lanka, I'd come over and visit. Who knows, maybe we'll find something worth exploring there!"

"Knowing you two, you will. And it'll be exciting!"

David smiled, "Yeah, you're probably right."

THE END

The Treasure of the River Kwai

The Treasure of the River Kwai

Order Form For:

The Treasure of the River Kwai!

Please print clearly.

Name: _____

Address: _____

City: _____

State: _____ Zip: _____

Telephone: _____

E-mail: _____

_____ copies of book @ $10.00 each $_____

Postage and handling @ $1.50 per book $_____

Total amount enclosed $_____

Make checks payable to:

Globe Publishing
P.O. Box 3040
Pensacola, FL 32516

Telephone orders: 850.453.3453
Website orders: www.gme.org
(most major credit cards accepted)

The Treasure of the River Kwai

The Treasure of the River Kwai

Order Form For:

The Treasure of the *River Kwai!*

Please print clearly.

Name: _____

Address: _____

City: _____

State: _____ Zip: _____

Telephone: _____

Email: _____

_____ copies of book @ $10.00 each $_____

Postage and handling @ $1.50 per book $_____

Total amount enclosed $_____

Make checks payable to:

Globe Publishing
P.O. Box 3040
Pensacola, FL 32516

Telephone orders: 850.453.3453
Website orders: www.gme.org
(most major credit cards accepted)

The Treasure of the River Kwai